S0-AEN-772

"You keep looking at me and frowning, Jess. Is something wrong?"

Abby shifted in her seat and sent Jess a bemused glance.

You are perfect, Jess thought grimly. *And I am in so much trouble.*

She flipped the visor back up. "Well?"

"I was just...checking the side mirrors," he muttered. "A habit from hauling the horse trailer."

The fabrication was ridiculous and Abby probably saw right through it, but what could he say—that she was the prettiest girl he'd ever seen in his life? And where would that lead?

A resounding shut-down, probably. And as much as he was tempted to tentatively test the waters, this could not be about him.

Betty desperately needed her help right now, and the twins did, too. Without Abby, Jess would be back to working 24/7, barely able to keep the ranch and house going.

Without her, he'd miss the banter.

The memories that kept slipping into his thoughts.

The niggling thought that maybe this time, he and Abby could get things right between them, if only he took it slow...

A *USA TODAY* bestselling and award-winning author of over thirty-five novels, **Roxanne Rustand** lives in the country with her husband and a menagerie of pets, including three horses, rescue dogs and cats. She has a master's in nutrition and is a clinical dietitian. *RT Book Reviews* nominated her for a Career Achievement Award, two of her books won their annual Reviewers' Choice Award and two others were nominees.

Books by Roxanne Rustand

Love Inspired

Rocky Mountain Ranch

Montana Mistletoe

Aspen Creek Crossroads

Winter Reunion
Second Chance Dad
The Single Dad's Redemption
An Aspen Creek Christmas
Falling for the Rancher

Rocky Mountain Heirs

The Loner's Thanksgiving Wish

Love Inspired Suspense

Big Sky Secrets

Fatal Burn
End Game
Murder at Granite Falls
Duty to Protect

Visit the Author Profile page at Harlequin.com for more titles.

Montana Mistletoe

Roxanne Rustand

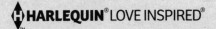

If you purchased this book without a cover you should be aware that this book is stolen property. It was reported as "unsold and destroyed" to the publisher, and neither the author nor the publisher has received any payment for this "stripped book."

Recycling programs
for this product may
not exist in your area.

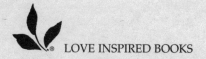 LOVE INSPIRED BOOKS

ISBN-13: 978-1-335-42843-1

Montana Mistletoe

Copyright © 2018 by Roxanne Rustand

All rights reserved. Except for use in any review, the reproduction or utilization of this work in whole or in part in any form by any electronic, mechanical or other means, now known or hereafter invented, including xerography, photocopying and recording, or in any information storage or retrieval system, is forbidden without the written permission of the editorial office, Love Inspired Books, 195 Broadway, New York, NY 10007 U.S.A.

This is a work of fiction. Names, characters, places and incidents are either the product of the author's imagination or are used fictitiously, and any resemblance to actual persons, living or dead, business establishments, events or locales is entirely coincidental.

This edition published by arrangement with Love Inspired Books.

® and TM are trademarks of Love Inspired Books, used under license. Trademarks indicated with ® are registered in the United States Patent and Trademark Office, the Canadian Intellectual Property Office and in other countries.

www.Harlequin.com

Printed in U.S.A.

Be careful for nothing; but in every thing by prayer and supplication with thanksgiving let your requests be made known unto God.

And the peace of God, which passeth all understanding, shall keep your hearts and minds through Christ Jesus.

Finally, brethren, whatsoever things are true, whatsoever things are honest, whatsoever things are just, whatsoever things are pure, whatsoever things are lovely, whatsoever things are of good report; if there be any virtue, and if there be any praise, think on these things.

Those things, which ye have both learned, and received, and heard, and seen in me, do: and the God of peace shall be with you.
—*Philippians* 4:6–9

With love and deep appreciation to my husband, Larry, for his never-ending support, and to our children and their spouses, Andy (Jenni), Brian (Julie) and Emily (Matthew), who are such a joy. I love you all beyond measure!

And also to Cheryl Kissling, RN. We were so very blessed by her comfort, support and gentle professionalism in the NICU years ago, when we lost our infant daughter, Christiana Leigh. Larry and I both felt we were held in the arms of an angel during those dark times, and I know that Cheryl's deep faith strengthened my own at a time when I felt devastated and lost. I now owe her additional thanks for providing medical information for this book.

Acknowledgments

Many thanks to Emily M. Vasquez, freelance content editor, for her suggestions and advice on developing this manuscript. Any errors are mine alone!

I would like to thank Bobbi Jo Crouse for her wonderful assistance with research questions on this book—and several previous books, as well.

Also, I would like to thank my Facebook friends for the times I've asked questions about conflicting research sources, and so many of them came forward with the right professional backgrounds or experiences to help me out.

Chapter One

Jess Langford stopped outside his grandmother's room at the rehab center and dropped to one knee. "Okay, girls. Do you remember what we talked about in the truck?"

The five-year-old twins bobbed their heads vigorously, their long, curly blond hair bouncing, though even now Sophie was edging toward the door, her bright blue eyes sparkling with excitement.

"We gotta be *real* quiet, so Gramma gets better and comes home." Bella wrapped a long strand of her silky hair around a forefinger. She was edging toward the door, too. "And we can't make her bed jiggly or she might cry. 'Cause she hurts."

Jess sighed as he stood. Betty wasn't hooked up to tubes and wires any longer, so those hazards were over, and she was made of much tougher stuff than anyone he knew. But the rambunctious twins had enough energy to wear anyone out—especially a seventy-seven-year-old woman who had been through surgery two weeks ago for a broken hip.

"Remember the rules? No running, no climbing on her bed. Promise? And indoor voices only, or we'll have to leave."

The girls raced into the dimly lit room and flung themselves against the side of the bed, chattering excitedly about their day in kindergarten. The pretty new layer of snow outside that looked like the sparkly *real diamonds* on their favorite Barbie dresses. Their latest adventures with their hay fort in the horse barn…which they currently called their princess castle.

Jess leaned against the door frame and stifled a yawn.

Last week, his only ranch hand had quit without warning, saying he'd had it with Montana's winters and was going back to South Texas, which left Jess alone to run a horse-and-cattle ranch. Amid all of that, he'd been taking care of the house, laundry, meals and the girls, and getting them off to school. These days, even four hours of sleep was a blessing.

But he hadn't been able to say *no* when Betty called at supper time and begged him to bring the girls for a visit tonight because she missed them so much. He owed Betty the moon and stars for all she did to keep the household running, so how could he refuse?

Seeing their joy and the love in Betty's eyes made the trip worthwhile every single time.

Jess straightened and moved to Betty's bedside to kiss her cheek. "How's my favorite grandma?" He teased. "Better since yesterday?"

"Getting better all the time," she retorted, spunky as ever. "I should be out of here in just a few days."

"I sure hope so. We all miss you."

He hadn't done much praying in years—he and God hadn't been on the best of speaking terms since his little sister, Heather, died when he was nine and his mom passed a year later, but since Betty's fall he'd been trying a lot harder. Hoping God was listening, he briefly closed his eyes and sent up yet another silent prayer for Betty's full recovery.

From the other side of the bed, Bella craned her neck to look at something in the shadowed corner of the room. "Who are you?" she chirped.

Jess looked over his shoulder, expecting to see a nurse or a tech of some kind. A frisson of awareness ran through him when his gaze landed on a woman in jeans and a sweater sitting stiffly on the edge of an upholstered chair, not someone in blue hospital scrubs.

Though he couldn't make out her features, the

woman's long, honey-gold hair and slender build instantly sent him twelve years back into the past. "Abby?"

She rose slowly and stood there like a startled doe ready to flee, tension radiating from her. "Jess," she said quietly in the sweet, melodic voice that had haunted his dreams for years.

He blinked and swiveled his gaze to Betty's smug expression before turning back to the woman he'd once loved with all his heart. The heart she'd ripped out and crushed beneath her dainty Tony Lama boots. "What on earth are you doing here?"

"She's here because I want you to hire her," Betty announced. "I asked Norma and Frieda from the senior center to put notices all over town. This young gal saw one and she needs a job. So now you just need to find a new ranch hand and we'll have the help we need. Isn't this just perfect?"

Perfect. Not the word he'd use. He blinked again, shell-shocked, as a flood of bittersweet memories tumbled through his thoughts.

She'd tried to stand in the way of his dreams. She hadn't believed in him. And her unexpected defection had left wounds that took years to heal. And yet here she was, thinking she could waltz back into his life and work at his ranch.

Not in this lifetime.

"I...thought you were married," he managed after a long, tense silence. "Right after we broke up. Then you moved away. Chicago, right?"

She nodded, then tilted her head toward the twins and seemed to consider her words carefully. "Honestly, when I inquired about the job, Betty's phone number was on the flyer, but not her name. And I had *no* idea that it was at your ranch. I can see this isn't going to work out, so I'll just be on my way and—"

"No," Betty said sharply. "You two just need to get over whatever happened between you, and think of this as business." Her narrowed gaze swung between Abby and Jess. "I'm being discharged the day after tomorrow, which means I can come home. But I'll still need to be driven back into town for therapy a couple times a week, and I will *not* be capable of cooking, laundry, meals and caring for the girls. Not for months. Well into calving and foaling season, Jess, when you'll need to be outside 24/7. Abby says she'll gladly work until the summer—"

Abby's startled expression suggested that Betty's assumption about that length of time wasn't quite true, but Betty barreled on regardless.

"—and by then, I'll be in fine shape." Betty leveled a stern look at Jess, daring him to contradict her. "But without Abby's help, I am not going to come back to the ranch and be an even greater burden to you."

Yes, Jess needed help. But *Abby*? "I just don't think—"

The older woman folded her arms over her ample chest. "You haven't found anyone else to help out, and Abby is in a bit of a pickle. So if you don't hire her, I'll be moving to the senior citizens' home over in Waveland, where I'll be out of the way. For good."

"Gramma," Bella cried, scrambling up the side rails of the bed and curling up against Betty before Jess could stop her. "You hafta come home. Then our puppy can come home, too. *Please*."

Sophie's eyes filled with tears. "We *need* Gramma. I don't like it when she's gone."

Abby watched the girls for a moment, her expression inexplicably sad, then looked up at Jess. "This is awkward for both of us, but it's true that I could use a job for a few months, until I go back to graduate school. And it does sound like you need help."

Right now, caring for the girls and keeping his beloved grandmother out of that run-down senior housing project were more important than anything. And a day didn't go by that the girls didn't beg to get their puppy back from the neighbors— who had kindly taken him in when Betty got hurt and life turned upside down at the ranch.

Hiring Abby might be a temporary solution for all of those worries.

Yet, serious questions began piling up in Jess's mind. Questions that would best be asked away from the twins' all-too-curious ears. He'd already learned that they often heard things that he wished they hadn't, then asked awkward questions at exactly the wrong times.

Abby's father's ranch was just thirty-five miles away. So why hadn't *he* taken her in if she needed help? What had happened to her teaching career—and the man she'd married right after she broke up with Jess?

But more to the point…just what *sort* of trouble had she gotten herself into?

"Let's discuss this tomorrow while the girls are in school," he managed on a long sigh. He pulled a Broken Aspen Ranch business card from his wallet and handed it to Abby. "Maybe at Millie's Coffee Shop, two o'clock?"

She nodded.

"Just so you know, I always have a background check done on anyone hired at the ranch. *No* exceptions." Her eyes widened, and he realized how harsh his words must sound. "My lawyer insists on it."

He'd known her since first grade. He'd loved her once. Imagining her capable of serious wrongdoing was like imagining the twins' new puppy guilty of bank robbery.

But the day after their college graduation, Abby dumped him, and he'd learned a hard lesson. He hadn't truly known her as well as he'd thought.

"What's your last name now, by the way?"

"Halliday." Her gaze met his briefly, then she turned to rest a hand on Betty's arm. "Guess I might be seeing you later?"

"You will." Betty snorted. "Don't pay any attention to Jess. He's had a tough time of it since I got laid up, but he won't be this grumpy once he catches up on his sleep. I promise you that."

Grumpy wasn't exactly the word she'd use to describe Jess, Abby thought grimly as she carefully followed Betty and her cherry-red walker into the Langfords' sprawling ranch house two days later. Then she got Betty settled in her room for a little nap.

The trip home had worn Betty out, though she'd staunchly insisted that she would close her eyes for a few minutes and then be rarin' to go.

Unsure of what might happen job-wise after talking to Jess, Abby left her luggage in the trunk of her SUV; then, at Betty's suggestion, she explored the house a bit.

From the kitchen, a wide arched doorway led into an open-concept dining room that flowed into a large living room with a massive stone fireplace and leather furniture. Oversize windows filled the living room with natural light.

One hallway off the living room led to Betty's bedroom, the twins' room, then several guest rooms and a large bathroom, while another hallway led to a south wing that probably held the ranch office and Jess's quarters.

Abby glanced at her watch, made a pot of fresh coffee, then sat at the kitchen table with a cup of steaming brew and her ebook reader.

The promised meeting at the café hadn't worked out yesterday—Jess had cancelled because of some ranch emergency—but said she might as well come on out today since her background check was fine.

What had he thought—that she might've been hiding criminal tendencies all the years they'd known each other?

At the sound of heavy boots clomping up the back-porch steps leading into the mudroom off the kitchen, she took a long swallow of coffee.

Maybe this wasn't the most awful moment in her life, but it was definitely one of the most awkward. She'd never expected to see Jess Langford again. To be here as his potential employee was beyond imagination.

If she'd had any other viable option right now, she would have walked away from his condescending offer. But she'd scoured Pine Bend and the other tiny towns in the area to no avail.

Jess peeled off his heavy winter jacket and toed off his boots, then walked into the kitchen, giving her a brief nod on his way to the coffeepot. His face was somber, as if he, too, was finding this situation stressful and wanted to be anyplace but here.

"You look exhausted," she said, taking in the weary expression etched on his lean, tanned face and the sag of his broad shoulders.

Even after all the years apart, she felt an unexpected urge to envelop him in a long, comforting embrace. "Hard day?"

He leaned against the counter on one hip. "A long one, and it isn't over yet. Thanks for bringing Betty home, by the way. I didn't expect to have a cattle buyer stop by."

The deep, rich sound of his voice was as compelling now as it had been years ago. "No problem. So my background check was okay, apparently," she said dryly.

He gave a faint shrug. "Figured as much. But with Betty and the girls here, well… I can't afford another mistake."

She regarded him with surprise. "Growing up in this area, I thought most folks in ranch country knew each other well, going back generations."

"We once had to fire a ranch foreman. Do you remember Hal?"

Abby smiled. "I remember his daughter, Chloe. Sweet little girl—she followed your brother Devlin around like a puppy."

Jess nodded. "Her dad was a nice guy, but then we discovered he had bottles stashed all over and was drinking on the job. I felt bad when we had to let him go, but we just couldn't risk having him around the farm equipment."

"Or hauling cattle down the highway."

"Exactly. That was the last time this ranch will ever skip a background check and references— even for Mary Poppins."

"Well, no one could argue with you being careful at hiring a nanny. You're being a good father. Just as you should be."

"About that…" He took a long slug of coffee and paused, apparently sorting out his thoughts. "The twins aren't mine. Not yet, anyway. We have no idea what will happen."

At his dark, pensive expression, Abby waited for him to continue. She'd guessed he was widowed or divorced, and the thought that he'd found someone who was the true love of his life, instead of her, had made her inexplicably sad. But the possibility that those little girls had suffered loss and uncertainty was much worse.

"I got a call from Child Protective Services

in California last December," he continued. "A neighbor reported that young children in the adjacent apartment had been crying all night and into the next day. The girls were only four at the time. The landlord and a CPS social worker found them cowering in a locked closet, scared to death. No one else was there."

Abby closed her eyes, imagining their terror. "Those poor, sweet babies."

"They were so traumatized that they couldn't give any information, but they were hungry and dehydrated. The social worker suspected that they'd been alone for a good twenty-four hours."

Abby stared at him, feeling more than a little sick.

"Apparently my cousin Lindsey arrived just after the CPS social worker did. She insisted that she'd left the girls with her boyfriend, and he'd never left them alone before. She actually seemed frightened when the social worker tried to pressure her into giving his name."

Abby had seen more family dramas during her years as an inner-city teacher in Chicago than she'd ever thought possible, but it never failed to break her heart when helpless children suffered. "What a horrible situation."

"The social worker told her she would be assigned a caseworker and insisted on taking the names of some relatives. She warned Lindsey about the possibility of an emergency removal of the children if things didn't improve immediately. That's why we were called—to verify that the girls could be sent here, if necessary."

"Is that how the girls ended up here in Montana?"

Jess nodded. "Apparently Lindsey got into a fight with her boyfriend when he finally came back. He became violent, and she fled to a friend's place with the twins. She called Betty and asked if we could take the girls for a month or so. She wanted them out of state, probably worried she'd lose them for good if the CPS got involved again. Personally, I think she was also afraid the boyfriend might hurt them."

"What about Lindsey's parents?"

"Her mother—Betty's daughter—died soon after Lindsey was born. Her dad and new stepmother divorced years ago. Neither wanted anything to do with Lindsey or her kids when I contacted them last winter. And neither of them have ever called to ask how the twins are doing."

Abby felt her heart wrench. "So you're the twins' second cousin?"

"They just call me Uncle Jess."

"And they call their great-grandmother…"

"Grandma Betty."

"I'm so glad they had family who could take them in."

"I keep hoping we'll get a call from Lindsey so at least we'll know she's all right, but it's been over eleven months with no word. I filed a missing-persons report with the police in Los Angeles long ago and finally hired a private detective. But we still don't know where she is or if she's even alive."

Abby bit her lower lip, her heart aching for the motherless little girls. "It's all so sad."

"I'm telling you all of this in strict confidence, so you'll understand if the girls are moody or difficult sometimes. They haven't had an easy life." He sighed heavily. "We think Lindsey and her boyfriend left them alone more often than she would admit. You'll see that Bella is quite the guardian of her sister, and Sophie depends on her a lot."

"What if Lindsey does turn up again—or some guy claiming to be the twins' father—and tries to take them away?"

Jess's mouth flattened. "That thought keeps me awake at night. I would help her any way I can. But if she refused my help and took off with them, how safe would they be? What if we couldn't find her again, and she was into drugs, or running with a bad crowd?"

Like that violent boyfriend. Or worse. "I'm going to start adding the girls to my prayers. They've been so blessed to end up with you, Jess."

A brief smile crinkled the corners of his eyes. "I can't imagine life without them, even if they can be a handful at times."

The glimpse of his smile made her insides tighten and warmth rise into her cheekbones. Even after all these years, her reaction to him was as strong and instinctive as ever—which was going to make their working relationship even more awkward than she'd guessed.

Hiding her blush, she turned away toward the windows facing the barns and the foothills of the Rockies. "I don't know how you managed while Betty was gone."

"Working a hundred miles an hour while the girls were in school." Jess poured himself another cup of coffee and offered her a refill, but she shook her head. "Most years, cattle could still be on the higher range and stay fat and healthy there for another few weeks. But we got heavy, early snow in mid-October and it hasn't let up. They can't paw through it to get enough to eat."

"So you're already hauling hay to them?"

"Yep." He studied the contents of his coffee cup for a moment, then raised his gaze to hers. "Which adds hours to each day, but now the snow is too deep to reach them. As soon as I can, I need to drive that last herd down closer to the barns, where it's easier to keep them on hay. The rest of the cattle were already moved."

"Any leads for another ranch hand?"

"Not yet."

"No wonder you need help."

Jess settled into a chair opposite hers at the round, claw-foot oak table and wearily ran a hand through his thick, wavy black hair. "Even after Betty is back on her feet, I don't want her fussing over the cooking and housework. I'd like her to take it easy for the rest of her life."

"Good luck with that, because from what I remember of her, she never liked to sit still."

"True. But at least it would be her choice."

Again, a corner of his mouth kicked up into a grin, and once again her foolish heart skipped a beat.

She pressed her lips into a firm line, reining in the impulse to smile right back. She was pretty sure that the quickest way to lose this job would be to look like she was going to follow him around like a lovesick teenager, and she most *definitely* wasn't planning to do that.

He cleared his throat. "There's something else we need to discuss before we decide whether or not this will work out."

His piercing, silver-blue eyes focused on hers, until she suspected he could see into her deepest thoughts. She shifted uneasily in her chair.

"Betty hinted that you're in some sort of trouble."

"Not in any legal sense." And certainly nothing she wanted to discuss with Jess, of all people. "Just…a bit of financial stress. Not uncommon, these days."

He sat, quietly waiting.

The silence lengthened between them until she finally caved. "Alan—my ex-husband—had mild MS when we married, but it hasn't progressed much. He's an accountant and still perfectly capable of working, but he hasn't held a job for a long time. I worked whenever I could as a substitute teacher, so I could be available on the days he needed help."

"And then you finally left him?"

The hint of censure in Jess's voice set her teeth on edge. "No, Alan decided he loved his longtime physical therapist more than me and he filed for divorce in June. It wasn't too complicated, with no kids and few assets to divide. Living expenses and his health costs always took most of my income."

Jess frowned. "So now you're headed back to school?"

She regarded him sadly. There'd been a time when her greatest dream had been to stay right here and become Jess's wife. To spend the rest of her life with him. She'd never wanted to do anything else.

Breaking up with him had nearly destroyed her. Then Alan, a college friend, had caught her on the rebound while she still felt shattered and alone.

She'd mistaken comfort and kindness for love, and had ended up in almost twelve years of marriage that cured her of all her remaining foolish hopes of happily-ever-afters.

She would never again pin her hopes of happiness on some guy. Now she dreamed of doing something *more*.

"I want to devote the rest of my career to autism research, so I've applied to a number of PhD programs in Special Ed. I hope to start school either spring or fall semester."

He raised an eyebrow. "I'm impressed."

"Well, don't be," she said with a laugh. "I haven't been accepted yet. In the meantime, halfway through a school year isn't the best time to try to find a full-time teaching position, so I've been trying to pick up enough substitute-teaching jobs to make ends meet. I finally decided to ask my dad if I could help out on his ranch and stay with him for a few months."

Jess gave her a curious look. "But that didn't work out, apparently."

"He sent a very brief email saying I was welcome to come, so I showed up at his ranch a couple days ago. He hadn't bothered to tell me about his whirlwind romance with a woman only a few years older than me. Or that they'd raced off for a Las Vegas wedding and a honeymoon in Florida for two weeks. Apparently they'd just come home when I arrived. Dad was out hauling cattle, but his wife was there and she was not very friendly."

She realized she was starting to babble, but couldn't seem to stop.

The whole weird deal with Dad and his new wife had been ricocheting through her head since that brief, awkward visit. What would a pretty young thing like Darla want with an old duffer like Dad? His money? He dressed like a grizzled old cowboy with a few dollars in his pocket, but he'd built his Shy Creek Ranch into a successful Angus-breeding operation, and West Coast investors had driven up the price of ranch land in recent years. He ought to be financially secure into old age unless something went terribly wrong.

"It was very apparent that his bride doesn't want me around, interrupting her marital bliss."

Jess's lips twitched. "I suppose that would be a problem, with his adult daughter hanging around."

The touch of amusement in his voice gave her hope. "I obviously can't stay there now that Dad has remarried. But I'd like to be in the area for a while so I can at least check up on—I mean, visit him. Without a job, I'll need to leave and try to find work somewhere else."

Jess took another swallow of coffee. At the troubled emotions playing across his handsome face, she reached for her car keys on the table and started to rise. "I understand this is a difficult situation. You can tell Betty that I changed my mind about the job so she doesn't blame you."

She was almost to the door when he called out her name.

She turned back to him with mixed feelings of relief and dread. Given their past, it would be so much easier to just walk away. Maybe she could find a waitress job in Billings or Laramie or Denver if she couldn't find enough substitute teaching days there...

"This is probably a mistake, but we both know it's nothing personal—just a business arrangement between two adults. Right?"

Relief started to bubble through her. "Of course."

He handed her a piece of paper. "Here's the advertisement I've been running in the Montana newspapers and a cattleman's magazine, listing the expected duties and qualifications."

She picked up the document and scanned the list. "This seems reasonable enough. I'm not a gourmet cook, but no one will starve. As for the rest, no problem."

Jess lifted a brow but apparently decided she had to be kidding about her cooking, because he quoted a salary that was more than generous.

She felt an inward sigh of relief. Now she had a place to live and an income to keep up with her bills.

Best of all, she'd be close enough to visit Dad's

ranch now and then. He'd always been the strong, silent, reclusive type, and maybe this would be a chance to finally grow closer…and also make sure he hadn't fallen for a woman planning to make off with his money.

But this temporary job would be nothing more than that. *Temporary.* She had no illusions about it becoming anything more.

Seeing the depth of Jess's love for his grandmother and those little girls, she knew he'd matured into a wonderful guy. His family was blessed to have someone like him in their lives.

But she already knew how little she'd mattered to him.

He'd broken her heart beyond healing years ago, when he adamantly decided to pursue a dangerous rodeo career despite her pleas to stay home and be safe. Her own brother, a bull rider, had been paralyzed for life while competing just the year before, and Abby had been terrified for Jess. But he still hadn't listened.

After the biggest argument they'd ever had, he'd chosen rodeo over her. Then he'd turned his back and walked away.

Chapter Two

Jess felt a surge of deep relief as he pulled to a stop on the highway and waited for the twins' school bus.

He'd been stunned at seeing Abby again, and more than a little hesitant to hire her, but in retrospect her unexpected arrival had been a godsend. After today, she'd be able to handle the bus-stop run and most everything else involving the house, the girls and Betty's needs during the day.

At least until he finally found the right permanent employee.

When Abby had stepped out of the shadows in Betty's hospital room, he'd been nearly overwhelmed by his attraction to her, the clench of his heart and a cascade of memories that came out of nowhere, threatening his equilibrium.

But seeing her had also catapulted him back to the last time they'd seen each other. The ultimatum she'd delivered. The wrenching pain he'd felt when she insisted that he give up his lifelong dream of a rodeo career that could help him finance vet school.

Dad had already said that more college was a waste of time and that he belonged back at the ranch—promising that he wouldn't get a penny for school. Vet school loans would have saddled Jess with crushing debt.

If Abby had really loved him, how could she have tried to force him to give up what he wanted so badly? After his state championships in high school and college rodeo, she should have known that he had a good chance of making his dreams come true.

They'd broken up.

He'd done what he wanted.

Yet just a year later, the irony of his decision bit deep. Dad got sick, and Jess had had to give up those dreams. Out of deep sense of responsibility and duty to family, he'd ended up back at the ranch anyway. And Abby was long gone.

The bright orange school bus appeared around the bend and pulled to a stop in front of his pickup, discharged the twins and then rumbled on down the road.

Clad in identical puffy pink winter jackets, with matching pink woolen caps and mittens, at this distance their only obvious differences were their snow boots…or lack thereof.

Jess leaned down for hugs. "I'm so happy to see you," he exclaimed as he stepped back, giving each a playful tap on the nose with a forefinger. He dropped his gaze to Bella's purple boots, then to Sophie's tennis shoes, which were nearly invisible in the ankle-deep snow. "But where are your boots?"

"She forgot them at school," Bella announced. "Again."

At Sophie's worried expression, he cracked a smile as he swept her up into his arms to brush the snow from her shoes, then put her in her booster seat, then hoisted Bella in. "Seat belts, ladies."

Once they were fastened in, he settled behind the steering wheel and looked up at them in the rearview mirror. "I've got a surprise for you back at the house, girls."

Sophie's eyes opened wide. "Presents?" she breathed. "Like Christmas?"

"No, not like Christmas. Sorry. Christmas is still how many weeks away?"

"Seven," Bella said glumly. "It's too far."

They'd become so impatient that he'd started looking at the calendar with them every evening before bedtime, counting down the days until the holiday. Despite their mother's troubled life, she must have managed some happy Christmas memories with the girls.

"You're right. Seven whole weeks, and Thanksgiving has to come first. But who's been away for almost a month?"

"Gramma!" The twins squealed in unison.

"Right. She's home now, but remember—she's weak and tired, and we can't be too exuberant."

"Zoober mint?"

"Exuberant. I mean that we don't want to act too excited. So just like at the rehab center, we can't climb all over her lap, or bump her and make her fall. Then she'd have to go back to the hospital again."

Chastened, the girls fell back against their seats.

"But there's someone else at the house to see you," he continued, glancing at the rearview mirror again.

The twins sat frozen, their eyes big and round.

"Mommy?" Bella whispered, her voice rising with heartbreaking hope and excitement. "Did our mommy come back?"

Jess chastised himself for such a blunder. "No, not yet. Do you remember the pretty lady you met in Grandma's room a couple nights ago? She had blond hair like yours and she was really nice."

Silence.

"Her name is Abby, and she's staying with us

for a while. She's going to help Grandma with the house and the cooking and with you girls, too. Won't that be great?"

When he looked up in the rearview mirror, he could see silent tears tracing down Sophie's winter-pink cheeks.

Bella's head was bowed. "When will Mommy come back?" she whispered. "She said she would come back. We don't want a different mommy."

No worries on that score.

He'd been too busy with the twins and the ranch to even think about dating.

And as far as Abby was concerned, that was a no-brainer. They'd had a long relationship but it had ended long ago. The sooner he found a permanent housekeeper the better, because then she could be on her way.

Yet he couldn't deny that it was a relief having *someone* to temporarily help watch over the twins and keep them safe.

He'd loved them from the day they showed up in Montana, so scared and lost and innocent, but they'd also made him face the biggest fear in his life, and he hadn't had a good night's sleep since they arrived.

He knew all too well how impetuous little ones could be. How tragedies could strike in an instant.

And how devastating it was when the fault was his.

* * *

Eager to get dinner started, Abby sorted through the kitchen cupboards and walk-in pantry, then mentally cataloged the contents of the refrigerator. She'd already gone through the chest freezer in the basement and found plenty of beef—which was no surprise on a cattle ranch.

Betty hadn't emerged from her long nap yet. And Jess had been outside in the barns all afternoon, only popping in to say he was heading out to pick up the twins.

The days were shorter now, in these first few days of November, and daylight was already fading, sending long shadows across the kitchen floor. She turned on the lights, then glanced at the clock on the stove.

She pulled a roast from the bottom freezer drawer and put it in the fridge for the following night, then tossed a couple pounds of ground beef into the microwave on Defrost.

She suddenly heard footsteps come up the stairs to the back porch and she turned to find Jess ushering the twins though the door.

She offered them a warm smile. "I'm so happy to see you girls again. How was school today?"

They silently stamped the snow from their feet and shrugged off their coats, hanging them up on a set of lower pegs in the entryway, and left their hats and mittens on a shelf above the pegs. Neither of them glanced her way.

"Hmm. I wonder if I have your names right." She looked at Bella and playfully tilted her head. "You must be… Sophie."

Instead of smiling, Bella turned away.

"And…*you* must be Bella," she said to Sophie. "Am I right?"

With an almost imperceptible shake of her head, Sophie pulled off her sodden tennis shoes and trudged across the floor, her socks leaving a trail of wet footprints. Bella followed her, giving Abby a wide berth.

"Go put on dry socks or your slippers, Sophie," Jess called after her as he hung up his own coat. "I'm afraid they were hoping their mom had arrived, after I told them someone new was here at the ranch."

Abby could only imagine how hard it must have been for them to find their mother wasn't here after all. "I'm afraid I'm an awfully big letdown."

"They'll come around. Suppers have been really basic since Betty fell, so I'm sure they'll be happy to see something besides spaghetti, hamburgers and frozen dinners."

Abby mentally readjusted her plans for dinner from spaghetti to meatloaf and baked potatoes, and lowered her voice. "Is there any chance you could adopt the twins?"

"From what I've read on the internet, they could be considered abandoned after no personal contact with their mother for six months. Now it's been almost a year."

"Is that what you'd like to do?"

Jess sighed. "I just want what's best for them *and* for Lindsey—if only I knew what that was. If she's still making a lot of bad decisions, they're better off with me. But what if she's in trouble somewhere? Injured? I want to help her, not break her heart."

"It's so ironic," Abby said wistfully. "You've taken in these sweet girls, and care so much for them. I wanted kids but my husband didn't. Alan was adamantly against it."

She'd always loved kids. They were the reason she'd gone into teaching, and she'd never regretted it. But years of longing for a child of her own had left a scarred, empty place in her heart that had grown with every passing year.

At the sound of small footsteps approaching, Abby turned toward the sound of a child coming through the arched doorway into the kitchen.

Bella and Sophie paused in the entryway, as if hesitating about what to say.

"Can we see Gramma now?" Belle said finally. "We'll be real good. Promise."

He glanced at the clock. "You can go down and peek in her room. If she's awakened from her nap, you can ask if you can come in. Okay? But don't wake her up."

The girls scampered away. "Gramma! You're home," they shouted as they ran down the hall.

Abby stifled a low laugh. "So much for Grandma's nap."

"I'd better get down there to referee." He glanced around the kitchen, taking in the spotless countertops and the floor Abby had swept and mopped while he was gone picking up the girls. "I'll always appreciate anything you do while you're here, but remember that what I care about most are the twins and Betty. They are my number one priority. Always." A flash of worry—or was it fear?—darted across his expression. "It takes only a blink of an eye for an accident to happen."

Why was he so worried? But maybe this was what it was like, when you were a parent with kids who could move almost fast as you could.

Betty would be good company and no problem at all; Abby was sure of that—unless the feisty lady started trying to do too much and Abby had to gently rein her in. But the girls were a different story.

She'd seen their wariness and resentment toward her and glimpsed the pain in their eyes. Those wounds were deep.

Now she knew there were just three things she needed to accomplish here. She needed to reconnect with her father and make sure he was all right. Bella and Sophie were going to feel happy and secure by the time she left.

And she needed to guard her heart against the cascade of memories and old dreams that kept tumbling into her thoughts. Of Jess, this ranch and all that might have been.

By nine o'clock that night, Abby had finished loading the dishwasher, wiped down the counters and leaned one hip against the stove to survey the kitchen.

The day could have been worse, though not by much. The twins had refused to touch the meatloaf, baked potatoes and glazed carrots she'd cooked. They'd even refused the cherry pie and ice cream, despite Betty's urging and the fact that Jess had wolfed down everything on his plate and asked for seconds.

They'd finally accepted the sandwiches Betty made before she limped back to her bedroom to turn in early.

And bath time wasn't a success either. They refused Abby's help entirely and Betty obviously couldn't kneel by the tub to help them. So Abby finally just sat by the tub, gave them washcloths and bars of soap, and wrapped each of them in fluffy towels when they were done.

Right now, Jess was in their room reading them

bedtime stories, probably wishing he hadn't bothered hiring her.

She turned at the sound of heavy footsteps that could only be Jess's. She took in the weary set of his shoulders and his jaw darkened by a five o'clock shadow as he entered the kitchen and headed for the coffeepot. "Are they all tucked in?"

He nodded. "I had a talk with them. They seem to understand that we need you here so I can get back to work and so Betty can get better."

As kindergartners, they were old enough to understand, though she wasn't going to expect full cooperation just yet. Not after the scowls and pouts she'd seen today. "We'll be fine. Promise."

At his doubtful expression, she smothered a laugh. "You forget—I worked as a substitute teacher for years. Often in middle schools, and we all know how tough kids that age can be with a sub. Do you remember those days?"

A flicker of a smile briefly touched his lean face, deepening the dimple in one cheek. Once upon a time, that smile had made her stomach flutter. It still hadn't lost its power.

He poured a cup of coffee, pulled his cell phone from his pocket and tapped the screen. "I asked a neighbor to come over in the morning to help me drive the cattle home. Fred says he can get here around nine, though I've been tracking the local weather on my phone and it sounds like we might be getting some ice and snow again."

"I saw that, too. Starting midmorning, if the forecasters are right. The local schools have already cancelled." She tilted her head. "Maybe you should start without him."

"There's almost two hundred head of cattle up there." He shot an impatient look at her over the rim of his coffee cup. "If I could do it on my own, I would've gone after them last week."

"I could help."

"And leave Betty alone with the girls?"

"Betty would be here in the house with them, and she could call our cell phones if there were any problems. How late do the girls sleep if there's no school?"

He frowned. "Eight or nine. Maybe. But I still think—"

"They're almost six years old, and they'll listen to Betty. She wouldn't need to do much—maybe give them cereal and toast." Abby shrugged. "And how long would it take to go after the cattle?"

"Over six miles round trip—though rounding them up and moving such a large herd will make the return trip take a lot longer."

"If we leave early enough we might even get back before the weather hits."

He finished the last of his coffee. "Do you still know how to ride a horse?"

"If I've forgotten that, I don't deserve to own a pair of boots," she shot back with a grin as he headed out of the kitchen.

True, it had been a long time. But at the thought of saddling up and bringing in a herd of cattle tomorrow, she couldn't contain her smile.

It would be just like the old days, a little voice whispered in her head. Her and Jess, moving cattle and working calves on the Langfords' ranch, or back at her dad's place. Trail riding up into the mountains. Heading off to the local horse shows. Sharing kisses and laughter in the moonlight during long rides after dark…

But it wouldn't really be like the old days. Not at all. Because this was just a business arrangement, and nothing more.

Chapter Three

The house was dark and still when Jess got up at 5:00 a.m. and looked out the back door.

No snow yet. But the weather app on his cell phone promised sleet, then ten to twelve inches of snow followed by forty-mile-an-hour winds gusting to fifty and temps plunging into the minus-teens.

Just what he needed right now.

Blizzards could drive the cattle to seek a windbreak. They could end up crowded into a tight mass in a corner of the fence, tails to the wind, unable to move any farther. A lot of them might die from the extreme weather and crowding.

It had happened several years ago, and his livestock losses had been heavy.

He walked to the mudroom and started pulling on his down parka. At a sound behind him, he turned in surprise to find Abby behind him with a big grin on her face.

Suddenly, the years fell away and it felt as if they've never been apart. Except back then, he would have pulled her into an embrace. Dropped kisses on her cheeks and the tip of her freckled nose. And the teasing and laughter would have been nonstop.

"I was just going outside to saddle up."

"Good. Did you talk to Betty last night about caring for the girls?" she asked as she reached for her own heavy down jacket.

He nodded as he pulled on his insulated boots, jammed heavy gloves into his pockets and donned his black Resistol. "I also texted Fred and said to check with me before he came over. I told him we were getting an earlier start, but if things didn't go well, I might still need him later."

"Blizzard coming. Two hundred cattle. What could possibly go wrong?" A brief, mischievous twinkle lit her eyes.

He'd discouraged Abby from helping him move the cattle this morning, but now he was relieved that she was this willing and ready to go.

"I didn't think you'd actually want to do this," he said ruefully. "It's not what you signed up for."

She swiftly pulled on her boots and gathered her gloves, scarf and hat. "This isn't my first blizzard, you know. And just think. If you'd hired some city-girl housekeeper, you'd have to do this all on your own."

She lifted a small, insulated duffel bag from a hook by the coats and grabbed two thermoses plus a stack of sandwiches in plastic bags from the counter behind her.

Surprised, he lifted a brow.

"Hot coffee and something to eat," she said as she placed the food in the duffle. "Just in case we run into trouble. Now, if you're ready, we'd better move. I have a feeling that weather is coming faster than we thought."

They were going out in bad weather after a large and possibly unpredictable herd of cattle. Under any other circumstances it would have been the antithesis of fun. Yet he couldn't help but love her take-charge attitude. Catch her sense of adventure. This was Abby, after all—the girl who had never backed down from a challenge and who had always been ready to try anything new.

For years, he had missed her. She'd carved such an empty place from his heart when she left. How was he ever going to keep from falling in love with her all over again—since he already knew she was going to leave?

The first faint blush of dawn had yet to edge above the eastern horizon as Jess and Abby jogged their horses through the knee-deep snow in one of the pastures behind the barns.

There was a heavy dampness in the air indicating that snow was heading their way, and his mare, Lucy, seemed to sense it, restlessly tossing her head and repeatedly breaking into an impatient sideways jog. Twice she tried to spin back toward the barn, but he corrected her and kept pushing on.

He'd put Abby on Bart, a solid cattle horse with years of experience, but the dropping barometer and bite in the air had Bart unsettled as well, and he'd thrown in a few feisty crowhops when they first left the barn.

He realized again just how much he'd missed her when Abby laughed and sat her bucking horse like he was an old easy chair, proof of her life growing up on a ranch.

She glanced over at him, her cheeks rosy, then nudged Bart into a slow lope, his hooves kicking up clouds of light snow, and Jess followed suit.

When the terrain grew more uneven and the pasture gate appeared up ahead, she slowed back to a jog. Twisting in her saddle, she braced a hand on the top of Bart's rump and grinned. "It has been *way* too long since I've been on a horse. Thanks, Jess."

He laughed. "Don't be thanking me just yet. We've got a long, long ways to go."

* * *

The wind started to pick up and light sleet was falling as they left the pasture and started down a mile of country road. Yesterday, the wind had sculpted monster snow drifts here, making it impossible to bring more hay out to the cattle.

Now the drifts had been blown about again, leveling off the highest mounds and leaving knee-high snow for the horses to trudge through. What this would be like once a heavy sheet of ice crusted the landscape and heavy snow followed on top of that, he could well imagine. If they didn't succeed at bringing the cattle back today, he'd have to arrange for a helicopter to drop hay to them—an expensive proposition that might not even be possible if the winds stayed high.

"You doing all right?" he called out to Abby.

Her face muffled by a long woolen scarf wrapped around her neck, she nodded and gave him a thumbs-up.

She had to be getting cold. *He* was getting cold, with sleet coating his jeans and slithering down the collar of his parka. But the horses were laboring enough as it was to break through the snow. He wouldn't push them to go faster.

Cloud-filtered daylight finally seeped across the landscape, turning the world into endless, blinding white, and he almost missed seeing the gate leading into the hayfield.

Abby rode up close to Lucy. "How far now?"

"About an hour to where the cattle are." He lifted a hand to brush away the slushy sleet on her jacket. "I'm hoping they're by the gate, waiting for their next hay delivery."

Abby patted the saddlebags tied behind the cantle of her saddle, where she'd stowed the duffel. "Hungry? Thirsty?"

"I just want to get this done and get home before the weather gets any worse. You?"

"Agree."

Jess moved his horse into a jog and then into a lope, and Abby followed in the trail he'd broken through the snow until they were through the hayfield and the terrain began to change, the land interrupted by stands of timber, with fallen trees to navigate and snow-mounded boulders strewn along the base of the rising hills.

Here the horses were cautious, heads low as they picked their way through the hazards.

Jess pulled to a stop and waited for Abby to come alongside him. "Still doing okay?"

"Fine." She leaned forward to scrape some of the icy slush from Bart's mane. "I'm just glad the temperature hasn't started dropping yet. We should be fine."

"The herd up here has been brought home for several spring calving seasons. Unless the changing weather has them nervous, they shouldn't be much of a challenge for you."

"Challenge? How quickly you forget," she said dryly. "I've been moving cattle since grade school. Let's get moving."

He hadn't forgotten. He'd just wanted to tease her and see if she'd smile.

Their similar backgrounds had attracted them to each other from the first day they'd met.

She'd started riding ponies bareback when she was three, and moved up to team penning and reining horses by the time she hit high school.

He'd once thought she was his perfect match. But how wrong he'd been.

By the time they neared the final gate, the wet, sloppy sleet was changing over to a thick blanket of snow and the temperature was dropping.

With the worsening weather and over six hundred acres of rough terrain to search, trying to round all the cows up would be nearly impossible if they were scattered.

God hadn't ever listened to his own prayers much, but he sure hoped Abby had been saying some prayers about finding those cattle.

"Do you see anything?" Abby shouted into the rising wind.

Just then, a curtain of snow swirled and lifted, and a huddle of cattle blanketed in white came into view. Bawling at the appearance of the horses, they pushed forward against the metal pipe gate, agitated, impatient and hungry for the hay they expected—but wouldn't get until they reached home.

Jess rode along the fence line in one direction and then the other, standing in his stirrups as he counted. "I'm guessing at least a hundred are here—but I can't see beyond the rise. I'll get a better count as they come through the gate."

Abby nodded. "I'll keep them together out here till you know for sure."

The cattle milled around and jostled each other as they poured through the gate.

According to Jess's count, three were missing. And those three could be anywhere. The chance of finding them was growing more slim by the minute.

With a sinking feeling in his stomach, Jess rode into the pasture and made ever widening loops as he hunted for the stragglers.

Nothing. Just snow and pine trees and absolute silence except for the wind keening through the branches overhead. *Please, Lord... Help me out, here. They could easily die in the coming blizzard.*

He needed to move the ones he already had down to safety. That made sense. The dollar value of a few, weighed against the value of the entire herd, wasn't nearly enough reason to delay, given the worsening storm. And yet, like the parable of the lost sheep, he just couldn't leave the last three out here to die if the blizzard grew worse and he couldn't get hay to them.

He pivoted Lucy back toward the gate.

"I'm going to look one last time," he called out to Abby.

She stood in her stirrups to look over his shoulder, then pointed. "Look."

Sure enough, a haphazard line of three head of cattle were just coming into view, trudging slowly toward the gate.

Agitated by the changing weather, the herd needed no encouragement to head toward home, where trees and the walls of the valley provided some protection. There, too, they'd find long loafing sheds angled to protect them from the prevailing winter winds and large round bales of hay waiting in the circular feeders.

After driving the cattle through the final gate, they rode to the main horse barn, dismounted and led the horses inside and down the wide cement aisle. The warmth of the barn and the bright overhead lights felt like a warm and welcome embrace.

"I'm glad to be back," he muttered. "How about you?"

"I'm just glad I got to go along. Thanks!"

Jess's jacket was weatherproof, but his jeans were frozen stiff and his feet were numb.

Abby, however, pulled off her stocking cap and strode merrily down the aisle ahead of him with

Bart, her ponytail swinging against the back of her red jacket as if she were still seventeen and ready for another adventure.

Just watching her made him feel like he'd stepped into the past.

She stopped in front of the tack-room door and looked over her shoulder. "Can I cross tie Bart here?"

"Yep." He stopped his mare at the previous set of cross ties. "The halters are just inside the door."

Except for where their saddles covered their backs, the horses were blanketed in snow, and their manes and tails were clumped with ice. Steam began rising from their thick winter coats in the warmth of the barn.

Abby slipped off Bart's bridle, put on his halter and hooked the two ropes hanging at either side of the aisle to it, then brought Jess a halter with a hopeful smile. "I can stick around for chores."

"Just go on to the house. But thanks. I couldn't have done it alone."

"No problem." Her expression crestfallen, she turned away. "Any time I can help with chores, I'd be glad to."

She disappeared through the door, leaving him feeling oddly unsettled.

Which made no sense.

Riding up into the hills with her today, facing the worsening elements, had reminded him of things he hadn't thought about for many years. The camaraderie that he'd never felt with anyone else. Their shared sense of adventure and determination.

And this morning, he'd felt that little thrill of anticipation that he'd always felt when he knew he'd be seeing her again soon.

It would have been far better to wait for Fred's help rather than to have awakened old emotions he had no business exploring, he realized with chagrin.

He'd have to be more careful in the future.

Chapter Four

She'd been running on pure adrenaline this morning while going after the cattle with Jess. The joy of being on horseback for the first time since she'd graduated from college, braving the elements and slipping back into her rancher's-daughter role had been exhilarating.

Working alongside Jess with real purpose once again had triggered memories of being twelve years younger with nothing but a bright future rolling out in front of her like a red carpet.

No disappointments...yet.

No misunderstandings or heartbreaks, or abrupt, wrenching changes in her life to catapult her in directions she'd never imagined. Her whole life had seemed as bright and new as that of a newborn foal back then, as limitless as the stars strewn across the sky.

That naive, youthful sense of being destined for

great adventures had certainly faded over time, yet here she was in Montana once again, single and free to go wherever her dreams led her.

After a long, hot shower, she felt as if her bones had dissolved to molten honey, but at the sound of the twins squabbling over something in the living room, she quickly pulled on her jeans and an old red sweatshirt and shuffled down the hall to the living room.

Betty sat in an upholstered chair, her eyes closed and her walker at her side. The girls were arguing over a Candy Land board game on the floor, with the colorful game pieces flung far and wide.

"Girls," Abby whispered, dropping to the floor next to them with a smile. "You need to be quiet. Your grandma is sleeping."

Both of them edged away from the game board, then got up and disappeared into their bedroom. Apparently neither of them had listened to Jess's remonstration last night.

"I'm just resting my eyes," Betty murmured. "It's all right."

"Thanks for staying out here while I took a shower. I can take over now if you'd like to go lie down."

Betty opened one eye and peered at her. "After the morning you had, you're the one who ought to go take a nap."

Abby smiled. "I doubt Jess is snoozing, so I don't need to either. Did he ever come up to the house after we got back?"

"Just for a quick sandwich. He won't be back in till dinner. Have you looked outside lately?"

Abby looked toward the wall of windows, bisected with a set of French doors, that faced the covered porch. Only a faint outline of the nearest pine tree was visible through the driving snow, and its branches were whipping in the wind. "Wow."

"Looks like we're getting everything the weatherman said and more. I set out some kerosene lanterns and candles in the kitchen in case our electricity goes. We've also got a couple cords of split firewood on the porch, so that always helps."

"What would you like me to do?"

"Get the fireplace going. I can't bend down to put the logs in, and it always feels so cozy in here with a fire crackling."

"Gladly." Abby rose and headed for the French doors. To the right, she could see a stack of firewood covered with a tarp. "What else?"

"Fill as many pitchers with water as you can find, in case the power goes out. While you were gone, I put a roast, potatoes, carrots and onions in the slow cooker, so at least that should be done for dinner." Her eyes twinkled. "Unless, of course, we lose our power."

"It already smells wonderful. But I really hope you didn't try to do too much while we were gone."

Betty waved a dismissive hand at her. "Only what I could. Maybe you and the girls can make biscuits and a dessert."

"Gladly." Abby retrieved an armload of firewood and knelt in front of the fireplace.

In a few minutes, cheery flames were dancing up through the fragrant wood, but she could hear the wind howling outside and just the sound made her shiver.

"Are you sure you wouldn't like to take a nice nap before dinner?" Abby offered her a hand.

"I'll catch a few winks right here." She settled deeper in her chair. "It's easier to stay right where I am."

Down the hall, Abby paused at the doorway to the girls' room. They'd pushed the door nearly shut, but left a sliver of it open. She knocked lightly. "Girls?"

They were talking and didn't hear her.

"I don't like her."

"Me neither," the other girl said glumly. "I heard Gramma talking on the phone. Abby used to be his girlfriend."

"What if she's like the lady with the black hair? Gramma said that one wants to marry Uncle Jess. Eeeuw. She always says we look like vegetables."

There was a long, painful silence.

"But if mommy comes, *she* can marry Uncle Jess and we can stay here forever. I don't want to leave."

Abby knocked louder, and pushed the door open a little wider. "Would anyone like to help me make biscuits?"

They fell silent. Bella traced the swirls of the carpet with her forefinger. Sophie picked at a loose thread on the hem of her jeans.

"Chocolate-chip cookies? Or a cake? When I was your age, I loved to help because then I got to lick the beaters afterwards." Abby gave a blissful sigh. "And that was always sooo good."

Neither responded.

"But maybe you two don't like cake or cookies," she added thoughtfully. "I could make…sauerkraut pudding. Or asparagus pie instead."

They looked up at her in horror, though when Abby couldn't quite contain a smile, Bella caught on and scowled up at her. "We don't wanna help."

"Your uncle Jess explained why I'm here, right?"

Bella looked away.

"'Cause Gramma's sick," Sophie whispered. "But we can take care of her. We're good helpers."

"Oh, I'm sure you're the very best," Abby agreed, opening the door a little wider. "If she asks you to do something, I'm sure you do it right away."

The girls exchanged guilty looks.

"But when you're in school, there's no one here to help her," Abby said sadly. "And making dinner can be awfully hard, with those heavy pots and pans. Right? And then there's laundry to do and beds to make. Grandma Betty is too weak to do all of that and Uncle Jess doesn't want you girls working that hard."

"But we could. We're big girls," Bella insisted.

"Yes, that's true. But he hired me to be here for a couple months, which isn't very long. While I'm here, do you think we could be friends?"

They didn't answer.

"Well, you girls have fun in here. I'm going to go make my *very* favorite cookies. If you want some, they'll be on the kitchen counter." Abby looked out their bedroom window at the deepening snow. "If you really want a special treat, we could even make snow ice cream."

Smiling at the puzzled looks on their faces, Abby headed for the kitchen.

They hadn't been impressed with her explanations, probably hadn't trusted that she would really leave, and with Betty as their grandmother, cookies were surely not a rare treat.

But she'd seen the curiosity and flicker of excitement over the possibility of snow ice cream, and perhaps that would be too enticing to miss.

At five o'clock Jess stamped the snow from his boots and came in the back door of the house. The scent of chocolate-chip cookies and the aroma of something wonderful emanating from the slow cooker made him even hungrier.

But the scene at the kitchen counter was far more captivating.

In a scene of domestic bliss, Abby stood at the counter in an apron, her blond hair in two neat braids trailing down her back, with the twins standing on chairs beside her. A heaping bowl of what looked like snow sat in front of them and the electric mixer was running on slow as Abby scooped in more of it.

"Is it working?" Bella exclaimed. "Is it ice cream now?"

Sophie tugged at Abby's apron. "Can we try it? Please?"

"It's getting a lot thicker, so it's almost done." Abby chuckled. "And yes, of course you can try it. Then we'll save the rest in the freezer for after dinner, and you can tell your grandma and Uncle Jess about how you made it."

Shucking off his boots and coat, Jess joined them at the counter. "What are you ladies up to?"

"It's a secret," Bella announced. "Don't look."

He held up both hands and backed away with a smile. "Okay—I'm not peeking. Will you show me later?"

Sophie nodded vigorously.

Abby glanced over her shoulder. "When would you like to eat dinner?"

"We usually eat at six, but it doesn't matter. I'd like to clean up first, though. It's been a long day."

"No problem." She scooped up two small bowls of the snow ice cream and watched the girls as they savored their first bite.

When she handed Jess a bowl, his hand grazed hers and he felt the warmth of her touch, which went straight through him.

She must have felt the same, because she abruptly turned away and he saw the tips of her ears turn pink.

"So, what do you girls think?" she asked, her voice a little shaky.

Enraptured, they finished their ice cream and eyed the big mixing bowl hopefully, but Abby just smiled. "No more right now—you can have some more after dinner."

They scampered off to the living room. Abby covered the bowl in foil and jockeyed it into the freezer.

"I haven't had snow ice cream since my mom died," Jess said as he tried a spoonful. "She always said a heavy, fresh snowfall was a blessing and we should never waste it. There was never a winter when she didn't keep plenty of cream and vanilla on hand—and the sugar, of course."

"It does look good. Out here, with no pollution—not even any neighbors—the snow is perfect. Even so, it has to be really deep, and I would never use it the next day."

"No problem there. I think we're up to fifteen inches already and it's still falling."

"Are we drifted in?"

"Definitely, until the snow stops and I get out the big John Deere. But I hear the wind is going to be high all night, so there's no point until tomorrow."

He snagged one of the chocolate-chip cookies from a plate on the counter. "Did you get them to help you with cookies, too?"

"No… We haven't quite made our peace, but the prospect of the mysterious snow ice cream drew them in."

"I'm glad the girls are doing better."

Abby suddenly lowered her voice. "You do know why they were upset, right?"

Jess frowned. "They were expecting their mom, but you were the new arrival instead."

"Partly. They really do love you, Jess, and they want to stay here. But they want their mom to come back and marry you so that can happen."

Jess felt his jaw drop. "Marry *Lindsey*? She's

my cousin. And not only is she way younger, she's pretty immature for her age."

Abby tilted her head in agreement. "They're worried that I might get in the way of their plans. They're also worried about some lady with black hair who seems to want to marry you, too. Apparently they overheard something Grandma Betty said about that, and they don't like this woman much. I believe they take offense to her calling them *vegetables*."

Aghast, he stared down at her. "I don't have *any* idea who they're talking about."

"My only guess is that she might have said something like they're two peas in a pod."

He rolled his eyes. "Must be Maura. She's an old friend who lives in town. We usually see her at church."

"Apparently you see her often enough that the girls are afraid wedding bells aren't far off," Abby teased. "Just thought you'd like to know."

"It's true that we dated now and then over the years. But when the twins arrived she said she wanted nothing to do with ever being a *secondhand mom* and that was the end of it as far as I'm concerned."

"No wedding bells, then."

"No. A few months ago she said she'd had second thoughts, but she'd already shown her true colors. Those girls deserve better."

He'd forgotten how easy it was to talk to Abby. Back when they were dating, they'd ridden together for hours and had never been at a loss for conversation. They'd talked for hours up in the hayloft at the ranch or her dad's.

Lost in thought, he absently took a bite of the cookie in his hand. Still-warm chocolate chips, white-chocolate chunks, toasted walnuts and pecans, all magically held together in a buttery-crisp cookie, melted in his mouth.

He slid her gaze over to her in awe. "Did you make these back when we were dating? If so, how could I have forgotten?"

Her smug smile made him laugh out loud.

"No. I spent years on a search for the most perfect chocolate-chip cookie ever and finally started combining recipes and tweaking ingredients on my own. What do you think?"

"If these aren't perfect, I don't know what is." He eyed her speculatively. "Sooo…do you share recipes? Say, like this one?"

"Only with my very best friends. So I'll have to do some very serious thinking on where you stand. But in the meantime, I'll make them whenever you want while I'm here."

He thought for a moment. "I seem to remember you warning me that you weren't a good cook. During our interview."

"I think I said I wasn't really a *gourmet* cook, but hoped no one would starve. There's a difference."

He found himself feeling at peace for the first time in way too long, and realized it was because Abby was here again, in this kitchen—with her sparkling eyes and delicious cookies and silvery laugh, her warmth and compassion and all of the things that hadn't been in his life for a long time.

He dragged a tired hand down his face as a sudden weariness settled over him like a heavy mantle.

"You look like you're going to fall asleep on your feet, Jess." She rested her small hand on his arm. "Go. Clean up and rest awhile. Dinner will be ready in an hour."

He hesitated, feeling there was something important he needed to say, but the words just didn't come.

Then he stumbled off to bed to close his eyes for just a few minutes before dinner…

Until a terrified scream awakened him at three in the morning.

Chapter Five

Startled by a scream, Abby jumped out of bed, threw on her robe and flew out into the hall, belatedly realizing she'd forgotten slippers. The floor was *cold*.

The house was dark. Totally dark. No glow of moonlight filtered through the blinds. Not even the night-light in the hallway was on. And the wind was even stronger now, battering the house with unrelenting force, rattling the shutters and scraping branches against the windows. It sounded as if some unknown creature was trying to break in.

The faint beam of a flashlight bobbed through the living room, and then Jess appeared in the hallway in a faded T-shirt and jeans, his haggard face a mask of concern.

A low, keening cry came from the twins' room.

"It's Sophie," he said in a hushed voice. "The power just went out and she's terrified of the dark."

It was no wonder, with what the poor child had been through back in California when she and Bella were left alone overnight.

He pressed his fingertips against the door to the girls' room. "Sweetheart, it's me," he whispered. "Uncle Jess. Can I come in?"

"It's *dark*," she wailed. "I need my light."

Abby waited at the open door while he set the flashlight on the bedside table so it illuminated the ceiling and softly lit the room. Bella stirred sleepily under her blankets, then rolled away from the light.

Jess picked up Sophie and sat on the edge of her bed, smoothing back her tousled hair. "Everything is fine. We've just got a snowy night and the power will be out for a while."

"Can't you fix it?" She turned her tear-streaked face up to look at him. "Please?"

"I just called the power company and they said it might be a couple hours."

"But Gramma has lights we can use. She said so."

"I don't feel safe using her candles or kerosene lamps when we're asleep, honey. Would you like to keep my flashlight?"

Her lower lip trembled. "I want you to stay. And I want our puppy back. Can you get him?"

He considered it for a moment. "Now that Abby is here to help us and Grandma's home, I'll go get him as soon as I can."

"Tonight? He could sleep on my bed."

"Tonight is too cold and snowy, but maybe tomorrow. It was nice of the neighbors to keep him for a while, wasn't it?"

She rubbed her eyes and yawned, then snuggled deeper into his arms.

Struck by the sweet intimacy of the moment, Abby felt her breath catch and a deep sense of longing wrapped around her heart.

Jess had been all she'd ever wished for back in high school and college. Fun. Daring. Smart. Someone who shared her love of horses and ranch life, dancing, and skiing on weekends. He seemed to excel at everything he ever tried, and she'd been proud to be with him.

But what she'd loved about him then had been superficial compared to what she was learning about him now. Seeing his warmth and gentleness with this distraught child made her imagine falling in love with him all over again, if she wasn't careful.

"What would you think about all of us going out by the fireplace for the rest of the night?" he continued. "With the furnace off it might be chilly by morning. We'll be warm and cozy out there."

Sophie nodded. "Bella, too?"

"Absolutely." He stood with her still in his arms and grabbed the quilts on her bed. "I'll come back to get her in a minute."

"I'll bring her," Abby offered. She leaned over Bella and touched her shoulder. "We're all going out to sleep by the fireplace. Would you like to join your sister and Jess?"

The child shifted and mumbled something in her sleep, then her eyes fluttered open. "I wanna go, too."

"Of course you do." Abby snagged her quilts and draped them over her shoulder, then scooped Bella into her arms. "Would you like to bring the pink sparkly bear on your bed?"

Bella nodded. "That's my best bear."

"Perfect. Let's go."

In the middle of the living room, two extra-long leather sofas faced each other in front of the fireplace; a third faced the fire. A couple of matching recliners and an upholstered rocking chair filled the room, while numerous wildlife prints and an elk-horn chandelier hung from the walls.

It was a warm and welcoming room, and much more upscale than how she remembered it years ago.

Abby helped Jess get the girls on the sofas, both snuggling with the extra quilts. The warm, flickering glow and gentle crackling of the fire lulled them back to sleep in minutes.

Jess hunkered in front of the fire and pushed some of the logs around, then added a few more. The flames highlighted the angles and planes of his face and limned his lean body with golden light, making her wish she had a camera to catch the perfect moment.

"What about your grandma? Do you think we should bring her out here, too, in case her room starts getting too cold?"

"She has the bedroom closest to the fireplace, so I think I'll just go open her door wide and cover her with another blanket. I hate to wake her, but if she stirs, I'll bring her out here."

He disappeared down the bedroom hallway for a few minutes, then returned and eyed the two empty sofas. He settled into one of the leather recliners. "This furniture is soft as marshmallows. I'm not sure it would be much support for her broken hip."

Abby curled up with an afghan on the sofa nearest his chair and surveyed the room. "It's a beautiful room, Jess. Just like out of a magazine. Did you do all of this decorating?"

A corner of his mouth briefly kicked up. "Nope. I know even less about decorating than I know about heart surgery."

"Your *dad* did it?" She remembered him as being tightfisted and short-tempered.

"Maura."

Abby tried to smother a grin. "Ahhh. Sounds like the twins might have reason to worry after all if the vegetable lady comes to call and decorates while she's here."

"That's her career. Her husband died young, and she needed income. So she started a decorating business in town."

"In Pine Bend?"

"Obviously there wouldn't ever be many clients around here, so she added a little florist and gift shop later." He rolled his head against the back of his chair to look at Abby. "After Dad died, I figured it wouldn't hurt to give her some business and help her out. Nothing in this house had changed since Mom passed away over twenty years ago."

Chastened, Abby lowered her gaze. "I'm sorry—I shouldn't have teased. And I really do think she did an amazing job here. I'm surprised she's not working in some upscale market in a city."

Closing his eyes, Jess gave a soft laugh devoid of humor. "Not everyone needs to move far away, Abby. Some find everything they want right in their own hometown…even if it takes them years to figure that out. Like me."

He was just starting to fall asleep when he heard Abby's soft, wistful voice.

"Do you remember when we were back in high school? Some of the neighbor kids would ride their horses over and we'd all play cavalry out in your pastures. Are any of them still around?"

"The Cavanaughs went bankrupt and moved away not long after their kids grew up. Dad swooped in and bought up their land for pennies on the dollar before any developers could grab it. He always figured my brothers and I would move back to take over the adjoining ranches and help build his Langford empire, but Devlin and Tate couldn't stay far enough away to suit them. None of us wanted to come home after college, really. Dad wasn't exactly easy to work for."

"But you came back. You could have found a way to pay for vet school and still follow your dreams, but you gave it up."

"Yeah, well… Dad was sick, and how could he have managed alone? Devlin is career military and Tate has done too well on the rodeo circuit to give that up. So I had to come back."

"You're a good man, Jess. I hope your dad appreciated what you sacrificed."

Jess's dad had considered Jess's return to the ranch his duty and privilege, not a sacrifice. And he'd remained as cantankerous as ever until the day he died. "Maybe this isn't the life I wished for, but it's been a good life. I wouldn't change a thing."

She fell silent for a moment. "What about the Nelsons—are they still around?"

"They went under, too. And Dad snapped up that ranch as well, just before his health started to fail. Drought and cattle prices have been devastating for a lot of folks around here."

"It's been tough for my dad, too." She tucked her feet beneath her and wrapped the afghan more snugly around her shoulders. "And he never really got over my brother's accident. Like your dad, he'd wanted his son to take over the ranch someday."

Her older brother had gone off to follow the rodeo circuit with big dreams but not much sense, and he'd spent more time on booze and women than he'd spent on his rodeo career. The consensus around town had been that Bobby's bull-riding accident was a terrible misfortune but not much of a surprise, given his wild, careless lifestyle.

"What's he doing now? I haven't seen him around here in years."

"Computer programming in Seattle. Still bitter about his wheelchair. I was so scared that something like that would happen to you, too," she said softly. "When I asked you to make a choice and you chose following the rodeo circuit instead of me, you broke my heart."

"And you broke mine when you gave me that ultimatum."

Back then, Jess had been young, fresh out of

college, and felt invincible despite the example of Bobby's accident years before. There'd been nothing he'd wanted more in life than to rodeo with his cousin Logan, earn money toward the massive cost of vet school, then set up a veterinary practice together.

"Ironic, isn't it?" He lifted his somber gaze to meet hers, silently acknowledging their broken past. "I started moving up in the ranks for the annual saddle bronc championship, but barely lasted a full season before Dad got sick and I had to come back to run the ranch anyway."

But no matter what had triggered that long-ago confrontation between them, it had only delayed the inevitable. When she'd *demanded* that he choose between her and his fledgling rodeo career, he'd seen the truth. She hadn't really cared about him or his lifelong dream to escape his difficult and demanding father and this ranch.

Earlier tonight he'd come in from the barn exhausted and cold clear down to his bones. The bright, welcoming warmth of the kitchen and the aromas of cookies and dinner had filled him with a sense of peace, as if finding Abby in his kitchen made him feel he was finally, truly home.

But whenever he thought of what might have been between them, he only had to remind himself that their once-in-a-lifetime love had only ever been in his imagination.

He might have loved her, but she'd never truly loved him back.

Chapter Six

Abby gingerly unfolded herself from the leather sofa, all too aware of her sore muscles after hours spent in the saddle yesterday, and tiptoed past the sleeping twins to add more logs to the dying fire.

Apparently Betty was still asleep in her room, but Jess was already up and out, and from the rumble of heavy equipment outside she guessed he was already moving snow.

She stood at the French doors and stared out into a world of white.

Bright sunshine had turned the glittering, crystalline landscape to a scene as familiar as a moonscape.

Drifts were banked up to the gutters on the south end of the house and had turned the vehicles outside into giant mounds of whipped cream. A convention of birds was gathered around the bird feeders out in the yard.

The house lights flickered on. Went dark. Then they came on again and she heard the furnace kick in.

Still, there'd be no school again today—of that she had no doubt—and the likelihood of taking Betty into town for her rehab appointment seemed pretty slim, unless Jess could clear the long lane out to the highway and the county graders came by in time.

She glanced around the room, noting the household chores that she could deal with this morning, then headed into the kitchen to start a pot of coffee. As soon as it was burbling away, she powered up the laptop she'd left on the counter and started looking through Pinterest for kindergarten-level art projects.

Whatever else happened today, she was going to do her best to win over those two little girls.

As if her thoughts had summoned them, she heard a rustle behind her and turned to find Bella standing just inside the kitchen, her long blond curls in a wild nimbus about her head.

"Where's Uncle Jess? And where's my gramma?" Bella demanded.

Abby looked at her and smiled. "Your uncle is outside clearing snow and Grandma Betty is still asleep. I think she's still pretty tired from her surgery and all she's been through."

Bella gave her a stony stare, and if this had been

a normal parent-child relationship, Abby would have gently called her on her poor manners. But this was a difficult situation.

Being dumped by a mother who hadn't bothered to stay in touch would hurt any child, and having Abby appear out of the blue had clearly been a most unwelcome surprise.

"Are you hungry? I'd love to make you breakfast."

The little girl fidgeted from one foot to the other, then looked back toward the living room, where her sister was probably still sleeping.

"Scrambled eggs? Waffles? Chocolate-chip pancakes? Cereal?"

Bella wavered, then gave a single stubborn shake of her head.

"It can be hard to decide. Maybe when your sister wakes up, she can decide what *she* wants and you might want some, too." Abby smiled. "In the meantime, I'm looking for fun projects we can do together. I found recipes for homemade playdough and finger paints. Or we could make some Christmas ornaments, if you'd like."

"Christmas is seven whole weeks away," Bella murmured, her face downcast. "I can't wait that long."

"I know exactly what you mean," Abby said with a sympathetic drop of her shoulders. "But there's lots of things we can do to get ready, even now. What about cookie decorating? We could make some Christmas cookies now and put them in the freezer."

Bella's eyebrows drew together in consternation. "And not eat any?"

"Well, of course we have to try them, right? To make sure they're good? In fact," Abby added thoughtfully, "maybe we could even decorate pretty cookies for Thanksgiving. I noticed a big box of cookie cutters on a top shelf, and maybe there are some nice turkey and pumpkin shapes."

"Yes, indeed. And we've got lots of decorating sugars and sprinkles in every color you can imagine." Betty pushed her walker into the kitchen and paused to give Bella's shoulders a squeeze before dropping gingerly into a kitchen chair. "I get them in bulk at an Amish village in the next county. Do you remember buying the Easter colors, Bella?"

The little girl shook her head.

"You and Sophie chose pink and purple and blue and yellow. And you did a mighty fine job of decorating, too."

Abby poured a cup of coffee and brought it over to Betty. "Did you sleep all right? Jess had the fireplace going last night, so he opened your bedroom door and brought you another blanket."

"Warm as toast."

Betty shifted awkwardly in her chair and Abby

frowned. "Are you uncomfortable? Do you need some of your pain medication?"

"I'm a tough old bird." Betty shooed her away. "Less I take of that stuff, the better."

"Speaking of that, I don't know if we can get to town for your physical therapy."

"No worries. A few days won't matter either way."

"Still…do you have the number of the clinic? I can call to see if they're open." Abby looked out the windows by the kitchen table. "Then I can check with Jess to find out if we can even get out of here."

"The phone number is on the red magnet on the fridge, upper right."

After making the call, Abby shoved the phone back into her pocket. "They're open for urgent care, but the physical therapist and her assistant can't make it in. So—what would you like for breakfast?"

Bella sidled next to Betty and whispered in her ear, then raced out to the living room.

"I guess I would like chocolate-chip pancakes," Betty said solemnly, with a sparkle in her eye. "And some bacon, too."

Abby listened to the girls playing for a moment, then moved closer to Betty and lowered her voice. "I hope I'm not prying, but maybe you can tell me something?"

Betty frowned up at her. "Of course, dear. Is something wrong?"

"When I first got here, Jess warned me that it can take only a blink of an eye for something bad to happen to little kids. Of course everyone knows that's true, but he... Well, he seemed almost paranoid about it. Did something happen to the twins after they arrived here?"

"No, but if anything happens to them—even just Band-Aid worthy—it's like another reminder of his worst nightmare. But he probably told you about that years ago."

Mystified, Abby shook her head.

"The boys were just nine, eight and six when their dad accidentally backed over their sister, Heather." Betty's eyes filled with tears. "She was only four."

Abby drew in a sharp breath. "That's *awful*."

"Yes, it was. Her death was a terrible tragedy." Betty's expression hardened. "Their dad was a mean old coot. He couldn't face what he'd done, and when it happened, he flew into a rage and blamed the boys for her death. Said they hadn't been watching her, and it was all their fault. He repeated that over and over until they believed it. But the thing is, they weren't anywhere nearby and they hadn't been told to watch her that day. He just hadn't looked before he stepped on the gas."

Abby's heart wrenched at how helpless the little boys would have been to defend themselves against their father's tirades. The nightmares they must have suffered. "Those poor kids."

"Less than a year later, their mama died—my youngest daughter. I know it was from a broken heart. And the boys? Not one of 'em is married. I think they were so emotionally damaged by their father that they never wanted to take responsibility for a family of their own."

Abby closed her eyes, thinking about how Jess had to somehow overcome those wounds and his fear to take in two little girls in need and had become such a loving substitute dad.

"Thank you, Betty, for telling me." Abby gave her a long hug. "It was a great loss for you, too, and I'm so sorry for all you've been through."

By the time the food was ready to serve, both of the girls were sitting at the table on either side of their grandmother and Jess was just coming through the back door.

His face was drawn and weary.

Abby looked up from flipping pancakes. "How is everything outside?"

"Better, now that the power is back on," he said as he shrugged out of his down jacket. "Chores are all done and I cleared the road to the highway so we can get out, but the county plow hasn't cleared the highway yet."

"Back when you boys were growing up, that

sometimes took a week or more," Betty said with a chuckle. "All winter I made sure our storeroom and freezer were stocked, just in case."

Jess toed off his boots and washed up before coming into the kitchen.

When he came to the table, his half smile revealed the dimple Abby had always loved. "Thanks again for helping move the cattle yesterday, Abby. No way I could've gotten hay to them after this storm."

"I enjoyed every minute." She brought the pancakes and bacon to the table, along with cheddar-cheese-scrambled eggs. She caught Jess watching her, his smile now reaching his eyes.

"You wouldn't be just a little saddle sore from yesterday, would you?"

Her gaze collided with his and held, and what started as a teasing look seemed to deepen into an awkward awareness that simmered between them.

She turned away to get the warmed maple syrup from the microwave. "No cowgirl is ever going to admit being saddle sore," she retorted, avoiding his eyes when she put the syrup and butter on the table. "Especially not one who was riding before she could walk."

"Okay...then I don't need to tell you that the ibuprofen is in the cupboard above the stove, right?"

Betty chuckled under her breath as she cut up

the girls' pancakes. "I've missed having an extra adult or two here. Keeps things lively, don't you think? All right, girls—bow your heads."

Everyone joined in the table prayer, then started eating.

"This is real good," Betty said with a smile. "Food always tastes better when I don't have to cook it. Aren't these pancakes yummy, girls?"

Bella gave her pancake a listless poke with her fork and pushed her plate away. "I don't like pancakes. Not with spots."

"Watch your manners, Bella. Those are chocolate chips and I believe Abby made them especially for you girls," Jess said in a low voice. "I think they are delicious."

Sophie looked between Jess and Bella, wavered, then put down her fork. "I'm not hungry. Can I go?"

"That's *'can I be excused.'* And the answer is no, Sophie. Not until you've eaten something on your plate." Jess gave the girls a warning look. "And that goes for you, too, Bella."

Bella flopped back in her chair, her expression mulish. After sliding a sideways glance at her sister, Sophie did the same.

Abby felt Jess's eyes on her and figured he was probably assessing her ability to handle the situation.

"Well. I was planning to make cookies this

morning with lots and lots of sprinkles, but I don't think the girls are interested. So instead, the girls and I could start cleaning the whole house," she said. "If we work hard, we could get it done by supper time, since it's too cold to play outside."

"Then they'd sure work up an appetite by lunchtime, since they don't seem to be hungry for breakfast," Betty said with a solemn nod of agreement. "Good idea."

The girls looked at them in horror, then resolutely started eating.

Abby smothered a laugh. One small battle won, though she knew that Bella's rebellious streak would have to be dealt with and that Sophie usually followed her sister's lead.

When everyone finished breakfast, Abby cleared the table and began loading the dishwasher.

"Are we making cookies next?" Sophie asked hopefully.

"We should go out to the barn first, because there's something I want you girls to see," Jess said. "It's nice and warm in there now that the electricity is back on. If Abby comes along, she can bring you back to the house when you're ready."

Excited, the girls raced for their coats.

Jess reached for a pair of pink leather cowboy boots on the top shelf above the coat pegs. "Use these, Sophie, since your snow boots are at school. I'll carry you out to the barn, okay?"

"I'm just going to sit in my favorite chair by the fire and read awhile," Betty said with a mysterious twinkle in her eye as she stood and grabbed the handles of her walker. "You girls can tell me all about what you find in the barn when you get back."

Abby refilled Betty's coffee cup and brought it to her once she'd settled comfortably in the living room with her Bible resting on her lap.

"You're a sweet girl, Abby," Betty murmured. "Always were. It was such a shame that you and Jess didn't end up together. Maybe someday…"

"Someday soon I'll be moving on." Abby grabbed an afghan and settled it around Betty's shoulders. "I want to try to spend time with my dad and his new wife while I'm here, but I hope to be back in school this fall."

"Jess tells me you want a PhD from some fancy college. That's wonderful, dear."

Abby laughed. "I have to wait to see if any of them accept me. Besides, Jess might find his perfect housekeeper any day. And then I'll be packing my bags."

Betty searched her face with an all-too-knowing look. "Things haven't been so easy for you all these years, have they?"

"I've been blessed in many ways. Really."

"Yet here you are. Without a home of your own, a family…"

"I'm just in transition and ready to start over." Abby smiled. "Somewhere."

"Somewhere could be *here,* my dear. If you and Jess just—"

Abby squeezed her hand gently and took a step back, suddenly realizing that the crafty matchmaker was probably trying her not-so-subtle ploys on Jess, as well.

No doubt the poor man had to be counting the days until somebody answered his housekeeper ads so Abby could be on her way.

Though with every passing day here, her uncertainty was growing. Did she *really* want to leave?

Chapter Seven

Jess carried Sophie out to the barn with Bella at his heels and set her down in the heated tack-room office.

It was utter chaos—but what else was new?

Clients coming to buy horses, drop off mares for breeding or bring their own in for training came in here to do their paperwork with Jess at the desk in the corner.

Those with training horses here stood at the big counter along the window with a cup of coffee or a Coke and watched him working their horses out in the arena. He prided himself on the tack room being a professional workspace.

Today, however, the girls' toy closet had to be empty, because there were dolls and doll clothes and crayons and paper everywhere, along with tiaras and sparkly princess gowns for dress-up.

"I guess we didn't get this cleaned up when you

girls were out here last." He glanced at his cell phone to check the time. "Do you think you can get it all picked up in a hurry?"

"But we're gonna play, Uncle Jess," Bella pleaded. "We can put it away later."

"Actually, you need to do it right now." At the sound of a distant, high-pitched whine of a motor, he shook his head. "And we need to hurry."

Both girls heaved a dramatic sigh but grabbed their toys and dolls and helped him put everything into the baskets and on the shelves in the closet. In a few minutes the room was clean once again.

The sound grew louder, then stopped just outside the barn.

"Who could that be?" Jess mused. "It must be Fred. Do you remember him?"

"He's the one who took away our puppy when Gramma got sick," Bella said glumly.

"Well, guess what?" Jess opened the tack-room door and went out to help Fred unstrap a small, blanket-covered carrier from the rear half of the snowmobile seat, then brought it inside. "Who do you think this is?"

Sophie's eyes rounded. "Poofy! Is it Poofy?"

The girls excitedly knelt next to the cage and squealed with joy when Jess lifted away the blankets. When he opened the cage door, a puffball of golden retriever fur burst out of the cage and headed straight for the girls, climbing all over them with sloppy puppy kisses.

Fred shuffled in and closed the door behind him. Almost indistinguishable in a heavy snowmobile suit, boots and a helmet, he pulled off his mittens and slapped them against his thigh, then removed his helmet, revealing a shock of white hair and his jolly face. "Looks like everyone is happy."

"Perfect timing." Jess reached out to shake the older man's hand. "Betty's home and we have a temporary housekeeper. I could've come to get him, though."

"Nah. You wouldn't have made it through those drifts with your truck or four-wheeler. Anyways, it felt kinda good to get out on the snowmobile before we head south for a week."

"Florida?"

"If the weather holds and the highways are cleared, we fly out on Monday."

"If your son has any trouble at your ranch while you're gone, just have him give me a call."

"Will do." Fred chuckled. "By the way, I heard about that new housekeeper of yours. An old girlfriend, eh?"

The rumor mill in Pine Bend was apparently alive and well.

"Abby and I dated a long time ago. But she'll only be here until I can find someone permanent."

"Hhmmpf." Fred gave him a knowing look. "I hear she's quite a gal."

The puppy began racing around the tack room, the girls laughing and chasing after him.

The door reopened and Abby stepped inside, her blond hair fanned over her bright red jacket and her cheeks rosy from the cold. The puppy darted for the escape route past her ankles but she swooped down and caught him just in time.

"Abby, this is Fred Baker, our neighbor," Jess said. "Fred, this is Abby Halliday."

"Mighty pleased to meet you." Fred winked at Abby as he pulled on his helmet and his heavy snowmobile mittens. "I'm sure I'll be seeing you again, young lady—unless that pup drives you crazy."

Feeling a blush climb up her cheeks, Abby held the wriggling puppy as she watched the elderly man go outside to his snowmobile. She was pretty sure Jess and his friend had been talking about her and she was just glad she hadn't arrived any sooner.

She held the adorable puppy at arm's length and looked into its shiny, black eyes. "Who is this—and what breed is he? He looks like a lamb in need of shearing."

"This is Poofy," Jess said. "His mom was a golden retriever, father unknown. That's what we were told at the animal shelter, anyway. His littermates were all different colors and some even had spots."

She turned the pup this way and that, admiring him. "Whatever he is, he's a sweetie, and quite young, I think."

"Ten weeks. We got him a couple weeks ago."

"I'm so impressed that you adopted him from a shelter." She eyed Jess over the puppy's downy head and suppressed a laugh. "And I think you figured out the perfect name for him, Jess. Good job."

He gave her a pained look. "The girls had that honor and I couldn't say no."

Yet another glimpse at what a kind and loving man he'd become. Bringing a new puppy into a family was never easy, and he'd already had his hands full as it was with the ranch and the twins. And it couldn't be easy calling the pup by name when other ranchers were around either.

Abby gently set the pup down and he took off again, playing some sort of puppy tag with the girls and skidding on the hardwood flooring beyond the area rug.

"So the neighbors have been taking care of him?"

"They came over to get him after Betty got hurt. It was just too difficult to give him enough attention." He looked as if he wanted to say something more, but then he turned away. "Girls, I need to start working the horses in the arena now, so I'm leaving you with Abby. Be good, okay?"

They were on the floor now, laughing as the puppy climbed all over them, and probably didn't register a word he said.

"They'll be fine."

He tipped his head in acknowledgment. "They have lots of toys in the closet, but the puppy will probably chew them all if he has a chance. There's a hay stall just down the aisle that the girls like to climb in, or you can take them back up to the house. The pup can go into his kennel in the laundry room if he needs a break from the girls for a while."

"No problem. Wait—can the girls be in any other parts of the barn, or just here?"

He hesitated at the door leading into the aisle. "Their pony is in the second stall down, and you can cross tie him in the aisle. They like to brush him and braid his tail and…uh…put pink ribbons in his mane."

"So he's a very patient pony, then."

"What my mom called a yard pony. A confidence builder. You could turn him loose in the yard with a kid on his back and he wouldn't stray more than a dozen feet in any direction. Only a nuclear bomb could make him move faster than a walk."

"Do they ride him?"

"In the arena, but always with helmets and close supervision. This spring I'm going to look for some ponies that are a bit more mobile than Lollipops."

Lollipops? Abby tried to suppress a laugh and failed. In all the time she'd known him, Jess had been a strong, resolute man's man who stood up for what he believed in and worked harder than anyone she knew. From his thick dark hair to the toes of his cowboy boots, he was more masculine and appealing than any guy she'd ever met, bar none.

And now his ranch was turning into a pink fairy castle, thanks to two five-year-old girls. It made her laugh—and it touched her heart in a way nothing had for a very long time.

"Before I forget—I need you to fill out a W-4 tax form in my office tonight, if you have a minute." After Jess shut the door behind him, she turned back to the girls, who were now sitting together in one of the club chairs, cuddling Poofy on their laps.

Yesterday she'd come through this room in a hurry. But now, with the twins happily occupied, she took time to look around.

The room was the size of a two-stall garage, with solid wood paneling. In the center lay a black-and-white-spotted cowhide area rug, with leather club chairs arranged around a large round coffee table. Trophy shelves filled one wall, flanking both sides of the large picture window looking out into the indoor arena.

She took it all in, realizing just how much she'd missed this world of horses, cattle and wide-open spaces during her years in Chicago.

The back wall was covered with saddle racks stacked four high and pegs for halters, bridles and myriad types of tack, all clean and neatly arranged. The glittering silver show saddles were on the top racks, protected by clear vinyl covers. The everyday working equipment was stored lower, within easy reach.

Moving to the window, she inhaled the familiar scents of fine leather and horse, and the fainter scents of hay and pine sawdust bedding that had drifted in from the barn aisle when Jess left through that door.

Enjoy this while you can, a small voice whispered through her thoughts.

She braced her hands on the granite counter installed under the length of the window and watched Jess work a young paint gelding with his usual patience.

The colt moved with a jog so slow it was nearly a walk, his head low and relaxed as he moved in smaller and smaller figure eights, then circles. Then a larger circle in an easy lope nearly as slow as his jog. A rollback. Off in the opposite direction in the correct lead.

Nicely done. *Very* nice.

Once upon a time it had been her in the saddle, bringing two-year-olds from gangly awkwardness to polished show horses.

A wave of nostalgia and regret over all the years she'd lost slid through her.

After Jess abruptly walked away from their relationship, she'd been heartbroken. *Bereft* was a better word—it had been like he'd ripped out her heart, and she'd felt an overwhelming emptiness.

But Alan had been there for her then—kind, steady Alan, who had stepped forward with a comforting shoulder, but none of the intense, passionate emotions that she'd felt for Jess.

And so she'd married Alan and moved to Chicago. Knowing that she couldn't bear ever seeing Jess again with his arm around someone else. Loving someone else.

But agreeing to a life with Alan had been shortsighted. Alan deserved better and she had, too.

The irony was that now Alan had found someone he loved deeply, and she was done taking chances. She'd decided she would rather be alone than ever go through that pain again.

Yet being around Jess—and being back in this world again—was starting to make her rethink her life…

Chapter Eight

After long hours of outside chores, Jess nearly fell asleep Saturday evening while reading princess storybooks to the girls at bedtime—much to their amusement, judging by their giggles and tickles.

Sure, he could've turned the bedtime stories over to Abby, but the request had died on his lips. How could he give up such precious minutes with them?

Fresh from their bath and dressed in warm, footed pajamas and matching purple robes, they smelled of soap and baby shampoo, and when they cuddled up on either side of him, it felt like the most important part of the day.

He never ceased to wonder how Lindsey could have left her girls in Montana as if they didn't matter. Didn't she realize how fragile life could be? What a huge blessing they were, and what a great responsibility she had for these girls?

Then again, maybe she'd found them overwhelming, and dropping them off had been an easy way to regain her freedom. She'd become the mother of twins as a young teenager. At twenty-one, maybe she'd come to the end of her rope.

Or something could have happened to her.

But surely she would have been found by now, he thought, firmly shoving that persistent voice aside. The police would have found *something*.

Once the girls were tucked in and their night-light switched on, he knocked softly on Betty's door and wished her good-night, then headed for his office, where he knew his stack of paperwork was growing taller every day.

His office. After almost a year since Dad died, those words still sounded strange.

Jess shook his head ruefully as he sauntered into the room and sat behind the massive oak desk. It all still seemed like Dad's. Little had changed beyond a better desk chair and a new computer.

The old landline phones were still connected, though, as well as the answering machine blinking impatiently on the desk.

Jess tapped the button and began listening to messages.

A nurse from Betty's doctor's office, checking on how she was adjusting being back home. The rehab office wanting Betty to reschedule her PT appointment.

At a soft knock on the door frame, he looked up to see Abby standing in the doorway. He waved her in, toward one of the chairs in front of his desk. He pushed a tax form across the desk for her to fill out.

He continued listening, jotting notes and erasing the messages.

Two prospective clients. One of Betty's friends from church. Maura's sultry voice, asking about the girls and Betty and wondering if he was ready to talk about redecorating his office.

He hit Erase.

"Uh… Jess?"

He froze at the sound of the familiar voice, his heart in his throat.

"This is Lindsey. I'm gonna…um…pick up the girls."

Not *my girls* or *Bella and Sophie* but *the girls*, as if they were simply property. No warmth, no loving eagerness.

The girls.

He pinched the bridge of his nose and closed his eyes as she continued.

"This is a borrowed phone, so you can't call me back." Her voice trembled. "I'm coming by Christmas, for sure. Or sooner. Things are…um… better. A lot better. I promise."

Reeling, he leaned back in his chair. It was such an unbelievably short message after all this time.

There was so was much she didn't say. And then all that she *did* say—as if trying to convince herself that everything was fine.

He didn't believe it for a minute.

From across the desk Abby's luminous blue eyes filled with concern. "Do you think she'll come?"

"Hold on a minute." He went to check on the girls to make sure they were fast asleep. The last thing he wanted was for Sophie and Bella to hear about their mother's message and then imagine she was on her way.

If she didn't show up, it would break their hearts.

If she did, it would break his.

Back in his office, he shut the door behind him and returned to his desk chair, then replayed Lindsey's message.

"Anything I can do?" Abby asked quietly.

"Don't say anything to the girls. Not yet." He flipped open his planner and marked the date of her call on his calendar. "What kind of life can she give them if she's still with that boyfriend? There was definitely something off in her message. It just didn't feel right."

He'd longed to hear from her someday, hoping he could help her get her life in order. But he'd also feared this moment since the day the girls arrived at the ranch. "Since she doesn't have a phone of her own, she probably doesn't have a job or a permanent place to stay. And from what the social worker in California said, she seems to run with bad company."

"Maybe she's trying to start over and wants to be a better mom this time," Abby ventured after a long pause, though it sounded like she didn't believe her own words any more than he did. "She's had almost a year to grow up."

Jess pushed away from his desk and started pacing the floor, too stressed to stand still. "The girls love their lacy, ruffled dresses. Sparkles on everything. Ribbons in their hair. Poofy and Lollipops and Grandma Betty. But when they arrived here, they didn't have a single change of clothes. They were *dirty*—as if they hadn't had a bath in several days. And there were faint bruises on their arms—like fingerprints, where Lindsey or her boyfriend might have grabbed them too roughly."

Abby's eyes shimmered. "If that boyfriend was abusive, he'd better not be around any longer."

"I sure hope not."

"Did you talk to the sheriff about what could be done? A lawyer?"

"Of course I did." He remembered the frustrations of those conversations all too well. "The sheriff was pushing seventy and about to retire, and he blew it all off. My former lawyer wasn't optimistic about any intervention either. He said that a mother holds all the cards unless there's obvious abuse."

"So what are you going to do?"

"I'd welcome Lindsey with open arms if she needs a home. But she'd better not show up with a dangerous boyfriend in tow."

Abby raised an eyebrow. "You probably feel like locking the ranch gates and barring the door."

"I'm not sure that would be any help, but it's an idea." He gave her a rueful half smile. "I'll tell Betty so she's prepared in case Lindsey suddenly appears. But like I said, I don't want the girls to know unless Lindsey is coming for sure."

"Of course not."

Jess felt like an anvil was pressing down on his chest, making it hard for him to breathe. "The courts would say Lindsey is plenty old enough to be married and responsible for a family. But the big question is whether or not she's even capable and can provide a safe home. If she intends to take her girls, I'll do everything I can legally to stand in her way, unless both of those answers are *yes*."

Late Sunday morning the county grader finally cleared the drifts on the rural highway running past the ranch, and Abby needed to go on a grocery run.

"Are you girls ready?" she asked for the third time.

They'd been romping around the house with

the puppy for the last half hour, but their smiles turned to sulky frowns at her request. Though their level of cooperation had improved somewhat, Abby knew the trip to town might include tantrums in the grocery store or refusal to stay at her side, and the trip was already making her feel weary.

Please, Lord—help me find a way to get through to them, so everything will go better.

It took fifteen minutes to get the puppy into his kennel and get the girls dressed in their winter gear, and another ten minutes to round them up from the tack room when she went out to the barn to tell Jess they were leaving.

By the time they got to town Abby had a headache pounding behind her temples that promised to last for hours.

She pulled to a stop in the parking lot of the only grocery store in town, switched off the ignition and prepared to do something she'd once promised herself she'd never do if she ever had kids of her own.

Bribe them.

"Here's the deal, girls. This won't take long if you stay close to me and behave. If you cooperate I'll get you each a treat. If you don't, no treat. Okay?"

Their expressions already promising trouble, Bella and Sophie unbuckled their car seats and hopped out of the SUV when Abbie opened their door.

An icy wind from the north was blowing steadily, kicking up clouds of snow underfoot. Abby took each girl by a mittened hand as she navigated the poorly cleared parking lot. Once inside, she helped them take off their mittens and hats.

She was barely halfway down the produce aisle, trying to gain the girls' cooperation with choosing apples and oranges, when she heard a gasp and looked up to see her new stepmother pushing a cart in the opposite direction with a teenager at her side.

Stunned, she stared—unable to find her voice. From the woman's rhinestone-studded silver leather jacket to her black leggings, silver-spangled knee-high boots and long fringe on her buckskin gloves—hardly warm enough for a Montana winter—it appeared that she'd purchased the entire outfit during her Las Vegas honeymoon.

Already spending Dad's money, Abby thought, before she silently reprimanded herself for being unkind. Maybe the woman had always been this… creative with her wardrobe.

"You're *still* in town?" The woman's viperish tone had not changed since they first met at Dad's ranch a week ago, nor had the oversize platinum blonde updo and heavy makeup. "I thought you'd be gone by now."

Who talked like that to a veritable stranger? To her new husband's daughter?

Taken aback, Abby struggled for a cordial answer. "I… I'm working at the Langford ranch." Just to test the situation, she decided to throw down a gauntlet. "But I plan to visit Dad as much as I can while I'm here."

The woman blanched, and Abby's suspicions about her intentions escalated.

Dad had never been one for flash and sparkle. He was a hardworking rancher who had simple tastes and very conservative views about money. So how had he ended up married to someone who dressed like a 1970s country singer? Was it possible that he was developing dementia and no longer himself?

Sophie tugged on Abby's hand. "She's pretty," she whispered loudly. "Like a cartoon princess!"

Abby gave Sophie's hand a reassuring squeeze, then lifted her gaze. "It's…nice to see you again, Diana."

"Darla." The woman paused, then exhaled heavily, as if giving in to the unpleasant situation. "This is my daughter, Lanna."

The girl—who was in her late teens, probably—wore black from head to toe, with long dark hair and a bored expression on her face.

With a flicker of shock, Abby realized that the girl was her new…stepsister?

Abby offered her hand. "So nice to meet you, Lanna. I'm Abby, Don's daughter. I hope we can get to know each other."

Lanna spared her a brief glance. "I'm not staying around here. This place sucks."

Darla sent her daughter a withering look, then turned back to Abby with an icy smile. "We're not sure about that yet. It's all been so…" Her eyes flared wide, as if she knew she'd said too much. "We're still deciding what's best."

With that, she shoved her empty cart to one side and headed for the exit with her sullen daughter in tow.

"Wow," Abby murmured to herself. So the marriage *had* been sudden. What had Dad gotten himself into?

But Bella and Sophie watched Darla's departure with expressions of pure awe.

"She's so pretty and sparkly," Sophie breathed.

"And she's married to your daddy." Bella's face scrunched up as she tried to sort this out with her five-year-old logic. She finally looked up at Abby in confusion. "Then she's your momma. But she's younger than you!"

Older, Abby guessed, but not by much. Mid-to-late thirties, probably. Which still put her at almost forty years younger than Dad.

Tomorrow afternoon Abby was going to go to her father's ranch and try to find out what was going on.

Chapter Nine

The skies were clear but the winds had picked up again on Sunday night, sending drifts across the highways and making travel too risky to try driving into town for church.

But by mid-Monday morning, the winds had calmed and the sun shone bright. The day seemed even brighter when Jess came in from morning chores and noticed two messages on the answering machine.

When he returned the first call and learned the only job applicant thus far for the ranch hand wouldn't be coming out for an interview this afternoon. He'd already been hired elsewhere. Apparently there were plenty of jobs around and far too few ranch hands to fill them.

Jess leaned back in his desk chair and spun it around to look out at the snowy landscape. Today the pine-covered foothills were visible, and beyond them the rugged peaks of the Rockies.

Even sleepy little Pine Bend was starting to show an increase in business because of the number of year-round tourists traveling through town on their way to the mountains.

The Millers, an Amish family with a ranch on the other side of town, had just opened the Amish Market & Café, which always seemed to have plenty of cars in its parking lot. And next to them, Maura's shop. Even with the increase in tourist traffic, most business owners had to diversify in such a small town surrounded by vast cattle ranches.

He could personally attest to that evolution. In just the past three weeks, he'd received several letters asking if he'd sell his ranch to developers.

Those letters had promptly disappeared in the shredder by his desk.

He turned back to his answering machine and listened to the next message. It was a woman asking about the housekeeping position. She hoped it did not involve any childcare, cooking or heavy cleaning. He rolled his eyes and hit the Erase button.

His ads clearly listed cooking, childcare and housework, forty hours a week, paid holidays and vacations. He'd tried to avoid misleading anyone, yet the few respondents had all taken issue with some aspect of the job.

After Betty broke her hip, he'd realized more than ever just how much hard work Grandma Betty had taken on when she moved in after Mom died. Life had quieted considerably after all three Langford boys had grown, but when the twins came she'd taken it all on once again—in her late seventies—without a word of complaint.

He was so grateful that Abby was here.

The thought popped up out of the blue and made him shake his head in wonder.

Never in a thousand years would he have imagined that he'd ever see her again—much less that she'd be working at the ranch. Living here. He felt as if he'd stepped back in time whenever he saw the familiar, mischievous twinkle in her eye or heard her laugh...or saw her sweet, gentle patience with the girls.

It was a blessing, and it was a temptation.

Would that long blond hair still be as silky if he sifted his fingertips through those waves? Would she still taste as sweet if he were to kiss her in the moonlight?

He wasn't going to find out.

He pushed away from his desk and found Betty at the kitchen table with her walker parked to one side, peeling and slicing apples. She looked up at him with a tired smile. "I feel like making apple crisp today. What do you think?"

He leaned down to kiss her temple. "I thought you were supposed to be taking it easy."

"This *is* taking it easy. Abby is busy with house-work and the girls. I love making desserts. I need something productive to do. Anyway, Mondays are too quiet with the girls back in school. Even Poofy thinks so."

The puppy, curled up on the rug in front of the sink, flicked his tail in a half-hearted wag at the sound of his name, then dropped his muzzle back down on his paws with a deep sigh.

"I just listened to some phone messages from job applicants a few minutes ago. Neither will work out."

Betty smiled up at him, clearly unconcerned. "No worries about anything here in the house. We've got Abby and she's doing fine. Don't you think?"

"For as long as she stays. But we both know—"

Her eyes narrowed, Betty waggled her paring knife in his direction. "Don't be wishing for change when what you've got is perfect, young man."

"Perfect for now," he conceded, wrapping an arm around her shoulder for a hug. "Have I ever told you how much I love you and appreciate all you've done for this family?"

She leaned into his embrace, then straightened

and started on another apple. "At least a thousand times. But this is my family, too, and that's what we all do. No one will ever love and care for us like family does."

He suppressed a sigh. He knew her next words by heart.

"That means you need to be more serious about finding a good mother for those girls. I won't be around forever," she said.

At this point she usually mentioned some lovely granddaughter of one of her friends from the ladies' social group at church.

But this time she just raised an eyebrow and fixed him with a stern look before picking up another apple. "By the way, Abby asked if she could run over to her dad's place for a bit after she takes me to and from physical therapy at eleven. She'll be back in time to meet the girls' school bus—if that's all right with you."

"Of course. Come to think of it, I'm not sure I ever discussed her days off. I'd better—"

"I get days off?" Abby walked into the kitchen with a laundry basket of folded towels on her hip. A corner of her mouth lifted into a teasing grin. "This I want to hear."

Abby pulled her SUV to a stop in the parking area between her dad's house and barns and let her childhood memories wash over her.

With caring for Alan and her substitute teaching, she'd been so busy, she hadn't been back to Montana in several years. But nothing had changed, as far as she could see.

The white ranch-style house still looked like it needed a coat of paint. The swaybacked wire fencing around the various cattle pens needed work.

Still, the cattle she could see looked fat and healthy and Tom, the grizzled old German shepherd watching her from the open door of the horse barn, looked like he'd never missed a meal.

A stranger driving in might assume the place was on the verge of foreclosure, but they would be wrong. Dad had always been as frugal as he was smart, and last she'd heard, he still ran five hundred head of fine Angus beef cows on the place.

Abby stood at the open door of her vehicle and scanned the buildings and pens. "Dad?" she called out. "Dad!"

When he didn't answer, she checked the machine shed and the barns, then walked around to look at the various pens.

She strolled back through the horse barn. It was empty now except for the two stalls in front for his ranch horses, the stalls festooned with heavy swaths of dusty cobwebs, the air heavy with the mustiness of abandoned spaces. She was nearly to the front walk door when it screeched open on rusty hinges and sunlight poured in, silhouetting a trim figure with all-too-familiar bouffant, up-swept hair.

"Can I help you?" Darla said sharply, her voice heavy with suspicion and a trace of fear. "What are you looking for—"

She broke off sharply when Abby reached the patch of sunlight.

"I'm looking for my dad."

Darla flicked a nervous glance over her shoulder as if she might be deciding to flee, and Abby wondered why she was so jumpy. "You should've called. He's…um…not here. But he'll be back soon. Very soon."

Abby doubted that very much. "Why don't I wait in the house, then. We can talk. Maybe over a cup of coffee?"

Darla fingered the long fringe hanging from the side of her gloves. "I—I don't think so. I have company coming. I need to get ready."

Dad must be around here someplace. Or maybe he'd gone to town. But he hadn't been here when Abby stopped by after first arriving in town either. Nagging concerns started sending icy tentacles slithering through Abby's midsection.

Dad was seventy-two. Five years younger than Betty, who was sharp as could be. She hoped he would enjoy another twenty years of good health and independence.

But what if he *was* failing, and being manipulated in some way? Held in his own home while his finances were being drained?

"Darla, I need to see my father. Now. His cell phone seems to have been disconnected. This is the second time I've stopped, and you've offered nothing but excuses both times. I'm worried about him. Where is he?"

Her gaze skittered away, not looking Abby in the eye. "I— He's in Billings. I can prove it."

"Show me. Because if you can't, maybe I'll have the sheriff check on his welfare for me."

Gone was the brittle, argumentative attitude Darla had displayed in the grocery store. Now the woman's shoulders slumped in defeat. "I guess you can come to the house."

Abby followed her to the back door leading into the kitchen. Here, too, nothing much had changed. The same cheap, dark paneling of a 1960s modular home. Conical brass lamps on the walls that pointed to the popcorn ceiling, which still sported heavy, fake wood beams that were really just Styrofoam.

It was past remodeling. It needed a bulldozer. Yet, the place seemed to be clean and tidy, with bare counters and no dirty dishes in the sink. There was no sign of her surly teenage daughter.

Darla waved Abby to a round oak table in the center of the kitchen and moved to a file cabinet at the end of the counter. After thumbing through some manila folders, she withdrew one and pulled out a bill of sale that she slid in front of Abby.

"Don is delivering a load of heifers to this man. He came here last month, chose which ones he wanted and asked to have them delivered this week."

She crossed her arms and took a step back, though she seemed to be regaining some of her spunk. "Satisfied?"

Not really, Abby thought, but if Dad was capable of hauling a load of cattle to another state, he still had to be pretty sharp. And if that were the case, then whatever he chose to do in his romantic life was his own business…as long as his new bride wasn't taking advantage of him in some way.

"I haven't seen my father in several years, and I miss him," Abby said quietly. "I'd like to visit with him while I'm still in the area. When will he be home?"

"If the weather holds, he'll be home late tomorrow night. Maybe midnight," Darla added.

"So he'll be here the next day?"

"Maybe. He's in and out a lot. You can call the house phone. That number got changed a month or so ago."

"That's odd. He had the same number for decades."

Darla's eyes darted to the door, then to the phone.

"There were bad calls. A lot. He…um…changed his cell number, too."

Bad calls? What did that mean? She'd have to ask Dad about it when she finally saw him.

Abby opened up her cell phone and tapped the new numbers into her Contacts as Darla recited them. "Thanks, Darla. I need to be on my way, but I hope you and I can visit the next time I'm here and get to know each other better."

From the woman's stony silence, Abby guessed she wouldn't like that at all.

Abby drove slowly down the snow-packed ranch lane to the highway, feeling both relieved and concerned. She turned on her blinker, then looked over her shoulder toward the house in the distance.

It was too far away to make out any details, but she had no doubt that Darla was still watching to make sure she was really leaving.

And was very glad to see her go.

Chapter Ten

Abby waited at the end of the ranch road for the twins' school bus, mulling over her conversation with Darla.

She knew full well it wasn't her right to judge others. She'd always tried to be open and fair to everyone she encountered, no matter who or what they were. *Judge not, lest you be judged.*

Yet the first time Abby stopped at the ranch on her way into town, with no knowledge of her father's recent marriage, the woman had been rude. In public, even.

But today, under that veneer of hostility—there had been something else. Fear. Which made no sense either. If Dad was going to be home on Wednesday she was definitely going back, because something just wasn't right. She could feel it.

Its lights blinking, the school bus crunched

through the snow at the mouth of the lane and pulled to a stop in front of Abby's SUV. She stepped outside and opened the back door for the girls.

The twins hurried down the steps but stopped and looked at each other.

The bus driver, a hefty white-haired man in coveralls and an unzipped Carhartt jacket, leaned over to peer out the door at Abby. "Who are you, missy? I don't recognize that car, or you either. And that's an out-of-state license plate to boot."

"I'm the new housekeeper at the Langford ranch."

He narrowed his eyes and studied her from head to toe, then looked at the twins. "And how I can I be sure of that? Do you gals know this lady?"

"Girls?" Abby prompted. They still wavered between cooperating and acting out, and she was never sure how'd they react.

Bella sullenly fiddled with a strap on her pink backpack. Sophie shot a worried look at her sister and dug the toe of her purple boot in the snow, following her lead as always.

The driver reached for a cell phone on the console next to him. "I can call the Langfords, you know. I'm responsible for these girls."

Abby nodded. "Yes, please do that. Jess is likely in the midst of riding some horse in the arena, and

Betty isn't driving yet. She said she would let the school know that I'll be doing this from now on, but she must have forgot."

The driver's stern expression relaxed, but he still made a quick call to confirm the situation. "Sorry, miss. I never take chances. Out here on an isolated road, anything could happen."

"I'm very glad that you're careful. Thanks." Abby shepherded the girls into the booster seats that she had switched to the back seat of her SUV, and slid behind the steering wheel.

Jess had asked her to come with him to the girls' school conference tomorrow after school, and she had demurred, not wanting to intrude or, worse, inadvertently hint to the teacher that her presence was of a more personal and permanent nature than it really was.

Now she realized that visiting with the teacher would be a good idea. If she had any chance to help these troubled girls, she would take it.

She looked up at them in the rearview mirror. "I know life has been really unsettled for you two, but it's time you tried to be a bit more cooperative. I'm only trying to make things easier for your Grandma Betty and Uncle Jess."

Bella's lower lip trembled.

"You're spoiling everything!"

"I'm what?"

"It's almost Christmas and Momma will come," Bella blurted. "Only maybe she won't 'cause *you're* here."

Oh, dear.

Had she somehow overhead the conversation about her mother on Saturday night? Jess had checked to make sure both girls were asleep, but still…

"Why do you think she will come at Christmas?" Abby asked cautiously. "Did someone tell you that?"

Bella's mouth tightened into a pout. "She *will* come. 'Cause that's when she brung us here. Last Christmas when we were four."

Abby chose her words carefully. "No one knows that for sure, honey. But if your mom comes someday, she'll be very happy that Jess and Betty and I have all been here to take good care of you."

Bella pointedly turned her head to look out the window.

"In the meantime, your Uncle Jess wants everyone to get along. And what you did just now with the bus driver was wrong. Do you understand that? You should have answered him."

Silence.

"Even if you don't want me here, you still need to obey. The bus driver believed you didn't know me and if he hadn't been able to reach Betty or Jess on his phone, what might have happened?"

In the rearview mirror, she could see the girls exchange furtive glances.

"He would've had to take you all the way back to town, to the school. Betty can't drive, so your uncle would've had to stop working and drive clear into town to pick you up."

"S-sorry," Sophie said, her head bowed.

A tear slid down Bella's cheek. Her shoulders slumped down in defeat. "I just want my momma," she whispered. "Me and Sophie want her for Christmas."

Abby's heart ached for them both…and for Jess, too. There were going to be no perfect answers, no solutions that left everyone unscathed.

She rested her forehead briefly on the top curve of the steering wheel. *Please, Lord, be with these children and the people who love them. Only You will know the perfect solution to this, so please guide everyone to do what is right.*

Funny how simply having Abby sitting next to him almost felt like a date.

It was already dark at five o'clock, the bright headlights of the truck cutting a swath through the pitch-black night and turning the snowbanks on either side of the road into mounds of glittering diamonds.

Waiting at a stop sign, he couldn't help looking over at her. Again.

Lit by the soft glow of the dashboard, her blond hair shimmered and her face seemed to have a lovely radiance.

She was still such a contradiction.

A true rancher, born and bred. Tough and capable and down-to-earth, at ease herding cattle for hours under the most extreme conditions, and likely more at-home in her boots than in heels, even after being away for years.

But she was also fascinating, and since she'd arrived he'd had a hard time keeping his eyes off her. And that, he knew, had to stop before he stepped into deeper waters.

She shifted in her seat and sent him a bemused glance, then tipped down the visor to check her face in the lighted mirror. "You keep looking at me and frowning. Is something wrong? Do I have toothpaste on my chin or something?"

I am in sooo much trouble, he thought grimly.

She flipped the visor back up. "Well?"

"I was just…checking the side mirrors," he muttered. "A habit, from hauling the horse trailer."

She probably saw right through it, but what could he say—that she was the prettiest girl he'd ever seen in his life? Where could that possibly lead?

Probably the sound of her swiftly packing her bags and her heading for the West Coast at the speed of light. And as much as he was tempted to test the waters, he couldn't.

Betty desperately needed Abby's help right now, and the twins did, too. Without her, he'd be back to working 24/7, barely able to keep everything going.

Without her, he'd miss the banter.

The memories that kept slipping into his thoughts.

The niggling thought that maybe this time, they could get things right between them...

He cleared his throat. "Speaking of trailers, I need to take some horses to Denver on Thursday. The owner wants me to help him work them on Friday morning so he can continue with their training progress. Or, as he says, at least avoid ruining them during the first week."

She laughed softly.

"So you'll be back late Friday night?"

"Should be. It's about an eight-or nine-hour trip, depending on traffic and the weather."

She brightened. "What should I do about the outside chores? Will you print up a list, or just show me?"

"The neighbor's son is coming over to take care of everything. No worries."

She gave him a crestfallen look. "I'd honestly enjoy doing it, if you ever do need me to help outside. Really."

"Someday, maybe—but not when it's the middle of winter and miserable outside." He pulled to a stop in the elementary-school parking lot. "Thanks for coming tonight. You might be able to offer insights about the girls that I can't."

"I'm happy to help in any way I can."

The snow hadn't been well cleared, and there were slippery, ice-crusted ruts crisscrossing the parking lot. Jess instinctively grabbed for Abby's arm when she started to fall.

In the past, he might have swung her around for a playful kiss at a moment like this. But the presence of parents coming and going through the school doors made him hesitate and the moment was lost.

"Whoa. Thanks." She laughed as she regained her balance. "Maybe I'd be better off waiting in the truck."

He looped his arm more snugly through hers and drew her closer. When they reached the school doors, he moved his hand to the back of her jacket to usher her inside. Did he feel her melt against him, or was it just him?

"We're right on time," he said, glancing up at a clock on the wall. "And this is the room. Mrs. Kelley."

A portly, middle-aged brunette with a wide smile and laughing eyes greeted Jess at the door with a handshake, then tilted her head and shook

Abby's hand, as well. "Let me guess. You must be Abby. Bella has mentioned you a few times."

Abby's smile faltered. "I'm almost afraid to hear what she might have said."

"Just that she wants her mother here instead of you. But that's perfectly understandable, so don't you worry. Change can be a bit difficult for little ones, and things will get better." The teacher waved them toward the circle of chairs she'd set up in front of a wall display of the children's artwork.

"In kindergarten, children don't yet have much of a filter," Mrs. Kelley continued as she settled onto one of the chairs. "So before we start, I suppose you know that the twins have been talking quite a bit about their mother lately. They tell the other children that she's coming back soon to get them, and I don't know how I should respond to that."

Jess exchanged glances with Abby. "I doubt it will happen."

"I know we talked about this at the beginning of the school year, and I've tried to be noncommittal about it, just as you asked me to. But…" Mrs. Kelley hesitated. "Bella is *sure* she'll be here at Christmas. I think she'll be a very sad little girl if that doesn't happen."

"All I can see is a huge disappointment ahead." Jess leaned forward, rested his elbows on his thighs and clasped his hands. "The girls have been with me since right after Christmas last year, and still she hasn't come to see them. She hasn't even called to talk to them on the phone. Can you imagine how heartbroken they'll be if she doesn't want to be with them on Christmas?"

Mrs. Kelley reached forward to rest a comforting hand on his forearm. "If that happens, they'll survive. I know they love you and Grandma Betty very much, and they're lucky to have you." She directed a comforting glance at Abby. "And I know you must be wonderful with them, too. They just need a little more time to adjust."

"Believe me, I know," Abby said with a soft, sad smile. "They want me to leave, thinking that then their mother will come back to stay. I'm trying to win them over, though."

"Abby grew up on a ranch nearby and has been a special-education teacher in Chicago," Jess said. "This fall she plans to go back to graduate school."

The older woman's eyes lit up. "Oh my. I wish we'd known about you last spring. Our special-ed teacher got married and left us midterm. It took months to find a replacement." She reached for a clipboard on the table behind her and scanned a checklist of topics. "Before I forget, I should warn you that the flu is going around school. It's a bad strain this year—a few of the kids have been out for an entire week. Have the girls been vaccinated?"

Jess nodded.

"Good. And you, too, I hope." She looked over at Abby.

Abby nodded.

"I suppose we'd better get back to talking about how the girls have been doing in school, right?"

Twenty minutes later, Jess had an armful of manila folders stuffed with art projects, spelling tests and simple math papers for each girl, and his mind was spinning.

"This sure isn't like the kindergarten I went to," he said when he and Abby climbed back into the truck.

She shot him an amused glance as she buckled her seat belt. "Times change. In the olden days, kids started learning the basics in kindergarten. Now, most of them have been in pre-K classes."

He snorted as he started the truck and turned up the heat. "I've got a master's in agricultural economics, but at this rate I worry I won't be able to help with their homework by the time they hit third grade and—"

The words caught in his throat. There was a good chance the girls wouldn't still be here if Lindsey did come after them. Just the thought made his heart feel as if it were starting to fracture.

"No matter what happens, you can be really proud of them, Jess," Abby said quietly. "And proud of what you've done for them. You heard their teacher say they were both very advanced for their age, right? And that they constantly need more challenging projects so they won't be bored?"

"It was a relief to hear that," he admitted. He shifted the truck into Drive and headed out of the parking lot. "I doubt Lindsey spent much time reading to them. They were barely able to sit still for a single book when they first came to the ranch."

"And now they want a dozen at a time, so you and Betty have done a great job." Abby fixed her eyes on the road ahead. "You've become a great dad, Jess."

He swallowed hard. "I can't stop thinking about Lindsey's promise to be here by Christmas. If this is the only Christmas the girls spend in Montana, I just want to give them the happiest memories possible. Something they can remember always—no matter what else happens."

He just wasn't sure how.

Chapter Eleven

On Wednesday morning, Abby helped Betty out of the car and walked beside her as she navigated her walker over a snowy curb and up the sidewalk. "Are you *sure* this is all right? I don't like leaving you here alone."

Betty hobbled into the rehab clinic with Abby at her side. Once Betty was checked in and her coat hung up, she settled gingerly into one of the waiting-room chairs. "This will work out perfectly, dear. I'll be here for about an hour of PT, and then Frieda is meeting me right here. We'll walk down to the Senior Center wing so we can visit over coffee, then we'll have lunch with our friends."

"You do have your cell phone, right? In case your plans change? I can come straight back."

"That's nice of you, dear. But just be back by three so we can pick up the girls at school." Betty patted Abby's hand. "Go on—the sooner you leave, the sooner you can have a nice visit with your father. I haven't seen him in years, so tell him hello from an old schoolmate." She leaned forward with a conspiratorial chuckle. "I always thought he was the cutest boy in school. If he'd been five years older, I might've asked him out."

Abby couldn't hold back her laughter. "Betty! You rascal."

Her smile wreathed her face in wrinkles, but the sweet beauty of it hadn't been diminished by the years. "I might've thought that, but you know he never had eyes for anyone but your dear mother."

Abby smiled, and memories of her parents came to mind as she drove south of town to her dad's Shy Creek Ranch, where she'd grown up.

This morning, she'd tried to play it safe by calling his cell phone. He didn't pick up, but she recognized his voice on the voice-mail recording so she left a message and then sent a text for good measure.

The house phone was another matter.

If Darla knew when she was coming, would no one be at home? Or would Dad's gimlet-eyed new bride storm out of the house when Abby arrived?

When she pulled up to the house, she surveyed the barns, wondering where Dad might be. Then she heard his German shepherd barking from inside the machine shed. A moment later Dad appeared, waved at her and then went back inside.

Quite a welcome after three years, but with the windchill hovering around minus ten, she didn't want to dawdle either.

"Shut the door," Dad barked from somewhere behind his 4020 John Deere tractor as soon as she stepped into the cavernous building. "Heat's on, and it's cold outside."

"I know, Dad," she said dryly. "Good to see you, too."

"Just hold on," he growled.

She heard a wrench hit the cement floor, her father grumbling, then the screech of metal on metal. A few minutes later he rounded the front of the 1960s tractor, wiping his hands with a dirty rag.

"I see you've still got the old girl running," she said, sliding her hand over its spotless flat-top fender.

He snorted. "No use buying new when the old one runs fine." He tossed the rag into a bucket on the cement floor and took an awkward step forward, as if planning to shake her hand—typical Dad—but stopped and held both greasy hands palm up. "Better not."

She took him in from head to foot. With so many questions to ask, where did she even start?

He had aged so much—beneath his Pine Bend

Grain Elevator ball cap there were short wisps of thin gray hair, and the deep lines in his face were now like ravines that spoke of a hard rancher's life spent out in the elements.

There was a gimp in his gait that she hadn't seen before when he motioned to a couple of tractor-seat bar stools in front of his workbench and settled onto the one next to a grimy electric coffee maker. A bad hip, maybe. Or a bum knee? She felt a pang in her heart at the visible evidence of his aging.

The coffee smelled old and bitter, and she shook her head when he offered her a mug before pouring one of his own.

"You're looking good, Dad," she ventured.

He shrugged off her compliment. "What's this about you divorcing that man and having no job? Maybe you should've found a job first."

She felt a flicker of relief at him remembering the letter she'd sent him, even if to Dad Alan had always been *that man*, a city slicker he'd never liked. But leave it to Dad to forgo all niceties and get right to the point. "Alan filed for divorce, not me. And I was the only one working. So now… I'm in transition."

"Unemployed, you mean."

Abby suddenly felt even more thankful that Jess had hired her. "Actually, I do have a job, on a ranch outside town. And in the fall I hope to be starting on my PhD in Special Education."

"Hmmph."

"Then I'll be a professor, Dad. I want to focus on autism research and make a difference in this world."

A grudging light of approval lit his eyes.

"So how are things here?" She lifted an eyebrow, hoping to get a rise out of him. "Switched over to Herefords yet?"

He sputtered over a sip of his coffee and shot her a look of disbelief. But then she saw the faintest deepening of the laugh lines framing the corners of his eyes.

"The day this ranch runs anything but Black Angus is the day I'll be six feet under."

She'd been worried about his mental status, but he certainly hadn't forgotten his lifelong prejudice about cattle, and she'd even detected a hint of humor beneath his usual crusty demeanor. All good signs. And for the first time, she wondered if she'd been misreading him all along. "I was wondering—"

The door to the steel building opened and a rush of cold air blew in.

Darla hurried over to Dad and threaded her arm protectively through the crook of his elbow. "Honey, it's time to go."

Dad looked at her in surprise.

"Remember? I have to pick up Lanna by three."

He still looked mystified, but then seemed to catch on to her urgent desire to whisk him away. "Not just yet, Sugar."

Sugar? Honey? Those words had sure never been in Dad's lexicon while Abby was growing up.

"No, now," Darla said plaintively, giving him an imploring look. "Greg is always so angry if I'm late, and I just can't bear it."

He covered her hand with his and dutifully slid off his stool. After a moment's hesitation, he awkwardly patted Abby's shoulder. "Maybe you can stop by another time, while you're still in these parts," he said gruffly.

Abby settled a long, assessing look on Darla, who was tugging at his hand. "I'll definitely be back, Dad, because I think we have a great deal to talk about. A very great deal."

Jess loaded a saddle into the rear tack compartment of his gooseneck horse trailer, then went back into the barn for a couple bales of hay.

Abby pulled her SUV next to his truck just as he was coming out with some extra winter blankets for the two horses he would be hauling to Denver.

"Well, the girls are off to school." She peered

into the tack compartment. "Looks like you're set for anything."

"This time of year you can't be too careful." He nodded toward the living quarters at the front of the trailer. "I've packed extra winter gear for my-self and stocked the kitchen, just in case."

She went to the side door and peeked inside. "Wow—this is really nice, Jess. How many does it sleep?"

"Supposedly eight—if they're hamsters. Com-fortably, probably just three adults. Go on in and take a tour if you'd like."

She came out a few moments later. "You've got everything you could need with that pretty little kitchen and a half bath. What time are you leaving?"

He glanced at his watch. "As soon as I get the horses loaded. Sounds like some bad weather will be moving through Colorado tonight, but if I leave now, I can beat it."

She bit her lower lip. "The girls are really wor-ried about you leaving. It seems like any change in the status quo makes them nervous."

"I know." He slammed the door of the tack compartment shut and locked it. "Are you going to be all right with them while I'm gone over-night? I know they aren't always easy."

"They don't *need* to be easy." She met his gaze squarely. "If I was that age and my mom had disappeared, I would feel insecure, too. But their gramma is here, and she's a familiar face. And I'll keep them entertained. Everything will be fine."

His eyes still locked on hers, he stilled, holding himself back from the most natural thing in the world—saying farewell with a quick embrace.

Maybe even with a longer one and a farewell kiss.

She seemed to feel the frozen moment of tension, too, because her eyes widened. Darkened. And then she abruptly stepped back.

"I'd…um…better get back up to the house to check on Betty. Have a wonderful trip."

She'd gone just a few steps when she pivoted and came back to rest a mittened hand against his chest and brush a swift kiss against his cheek. "Stay safe."

She was halfway to the house before he could react. But hours later, he still felt the warmth of that innocent kiss.

Chapter Twelve

"Are you sure you aren't hungry?" Abby finished filling a platter with fried chicken and brought it to the table. "I made this because I thought it was your favorite."

The twins watched her somberly from their places at the table as she placed a chicken leg on each of their plates, followed by a scoop of home-made mashed potatoes.

"And these are the mixed veggies that you like," Abby continued. "Aren't they pretty and bright?"

"Everything looks wonderful," Betty said loyally as she dished up her own plate. "We're all so lucky to have a good hot meal like this when there are so many folks who don't."

Abby took her place at the table and bowed her head. "Can we all say grace?"

The girls half-heartedly joined in, but then listlessly pushed their food around their plates. By the time Abby and Betty finished, they still hadn't eaten a bite.

"Hmm… Sophie, can you tell me about the best part of school today? Except lunch and recess."

"A girl threw up on the teacher," she said after a long pause. "And Mrs. Kelley had to go home 'cause her dress was yucky. So the principal came and read us stories."

Poor Mrs. Kelley. Not only dealing with influenza going through the class, but now a stomach virus, as well.

"So aside from that," Abby said dryly. "How about you, Bella? What was the best part of your day?"

Bella smeared her mashed potatoes across her plate. "Dunno."

Abby looked closer at the twins. Did they seem a bit pale? Unusually tired? Or were they just unsettled because Jess was gone? She caught Betty's eye, tipped her head in the twins' direction and frowned.

Betty nodded. "Do you know what, maybe we should have an earlier bath tonight, so everyone can be warm and snuggly in their pajamas. A good night's sleep would do everyone good, don't you think?"

Bella looked up in alarm. "What about stories?"

"Of course, we'll read stories," Abby said. "That's *my* favorite time of the day. Why don't you two pick out a nice stack, and I'll help you with your baths after I straighten up the kitchen."

The twins dutifully slid off their chairs and disappeared with the puppy at their heels.

"I can take care of the kitchen," Betty protested, awkwardly rising from her chair. "It's no bother."

"But it's my job, and I don't mind at all. Why don't you go enjoy the fire for a while? I got it started before dinner. I can bring you some decaf coffee if you'd like."

Betty pushed her walker toward the door, then turned back. "Have you heard anything from Jess?"

"No. Why?"

"I tried calling him and he didn't answer. I didn't want to say anything with the girls listening, but—" She lowered her voice. "On the news I heard about a bad weather system hitting much of Colorado. A good half inch of ice coating the highways and power lines and heavy snow on its way. Major pileups on the freeways."

Abby suddenly felt faint.

Jess had been hauling horses since he was a teenager, and she knew he was a safe driver.

But the other cars and trucks on the highway in dangerous conditions like that were always the wild cards if they were reckless, speeding or both.

Anything could happen.

Yet just hours ago she'd been standing with

him out in the driveway, talking so casually about his trip. She'd felt his heartbeat beneath her hand when she'd kissed him—something she hadn't been able to stop thinking about this entire day.

It was meant as a casual kiss between friends wishing each other well. Yet it had conjured up all sorts of feelings she'd been trying to avoid, given this oh-so-temporary situation.

She'd kissed him…then raced off like a scared bunny, not knowing if he'd had any reaction at all.

Abby shook off her thoughts. "H-he didn't say anything about planning to call tonight, but he did mention the weather. He thought he'd get there in plenty of time to avoid it."

Betty shook her head. "The newscaster said the weather system took a sharp turn, and the storm hit much earlier. Do let me know if you talk to him, okay? I don't dare call and distract him if he's still driving."

"Me neither." Abby felt a shiver work its way down her spine. "So I guess all we can do is pray."

Bath time, a dozen short storybooks and one declined bedtime snack later, Abby kissed the girls good-night, turned on their night-light and stepped out of their room. The soft glow of the hallway night-light lit her way to the living room, where she found Betty asleep in her favorite chair.

Abby debated about bothering her, then lightly touched her arm. "Wouldn't you be more comfortable in bed?"

"Was I sleeping?" Betty blinked and sat up a little straighter, then yawned. Her eyes widened. "Did you hear from Jess?"

Abby retrieved her cell phone from the kitchen and studied the screen. "No phone messages and no texts. I could send him one, but I'd rather not right now, just in case he…"

"Don't. He might still be driving in that mess."

Driving…or in a ditch somewhere.

He could be hurt.

Lying in a hospital. Or worse…

She said a quick, silent prayer and rallied a smile for Betty. "He probably already arrived and is out to dinner somewhere with his clients. I'm sure he's fine."

"But if you hear anything…"

"I will come to tell you. Promise." Abby helped her stand up and angled her walker into place. "If you're asleep, I'll leave you a note on your nightstand in case you wake up during the night. Okay?"

Betty squeezed her hand. "We're so lucky to have you here, dear. I just wonder if Jess realizes it. I need to have another talk with that boy."

Another talk? "Oh, Betty," Abby managed over

a strangled laugh. "I'd really rather you didn't. Promise me you won't. Please."

"Good night, sleep tight," Betty said over her shoulder.

Her enigmatic smile promised nothing, but Abby hoped she'd stop meddling. Any sly hints from her would only make this situation more awkward.

And besides, it would be a long, long time before Abby risked her heart again over any guy. What had she ever gotten out of it?

Her dad had influenced her relationships with men by mostly ignoring her while she was growing up.

Jess had chosen rodeos over her.

And then there was the unexpected discovery of Alan's infidelity, followed by the unexpected divorce.

Three strikes, and she was *out.*

And if Jess hadn't married in all these years, he most likely wasn't the marrying type.

Case closed.

Abby watched Betty slowly make her way down the hall to the bathroom; then she turned to the fireplace and pushed at the last glowing remnants with the fireplace poker. Flames shot up briefly with a shower of sparks, then faded.

After letting the puppy outside one last time and putting him in his kennel in the laundry room for the night, she wandered slowly through the living room as memories drifted through her thoughts.

The room had looked much different then, but the fireplace was the same as when she and Jess had come in after cool autumn afternoons outside, riding horses or moving cattle for his dad. They'd sometimes sat in front of the fire, idly talking about their dreams, thinking those days would never end.

A cloak of melancholy seemed to wrap around her shoulders as she thought about missed chances and lost dreams, and all the ways life could change with a simple fork of the road.

A faint cry drifted down the hall and she stilled, listening.

Sophie still suffered from random nightmares, owing to her fear of the dark, but that noise hadn't been her usual jagged scream.

Abby stilled, listening.

And it came again—like someone moaning in their sleep. She hurried down the hall and stopped at Betty's closed door, listened, then moved on to the twins' room.

The pretty little fairy night-light cast streams of pastel light up the walls and across both twin beds. Sophie seemed to be fast asleep, but it was Bella who was unsettled.

She'd thrashed away her blankets and curled up into a tight ball, hugging her pillow to her chest.

She moaned, then abruptly sat up and lost her supper—or what little of it she had eaten.

When she started to lie down again Abby caught her just in time. "Sweetie—we need to get you cleaned up and change your bedding, first."

Bella looked blearily up at her, her eyes unfocused. She felt hot, yet chills were shaking her little body. "I don't feel good," she whispered. "I hurt."

Abby rushed the damp strands of hair away from her feverish forehead. "Where do you hurt?"

"My head and all over. A lot."

"Well, we're going to take care of things and help you get better. Okay? We'll get you all cleaned up so you can try to get some sleep."

Abby helped her wash up, put her in fresh pajamas and changed her bed linens. Then she gave Bella some liquid pain reliever and went to gather some afghans and her pillow so she could sleep on the floor in the girls' room in case Bella got worse.

While saying farewell to Jess this morning, she'd been offhand about being able to handle everything. Tonight she realized she'd been wrong.

Without him here, she was responsible for everyone at this isolated ranch. An elderly, disabled woman, one sick child and another who would likely start showing symptoms anytime. She'd never again underestimate the job mothers did every single day.

And yet this is what Jess had been doing on his own until she turned up—looking after his family *plus* a full-time job dealing with everything outside. Her estimation of him rose tenfold.

And when he got home—God willing—she was going to tell him so.

Chapter Thirteen

Abby awoke to two small faces hanging over the edges of their twin beds, peering down at her.

Sophie frowned. "Did you sleep on our floor 'cause you had bad dreams?"

"No." Abby rolled over, every muscle and joint aching from the night—such as it was—that she'd spent on the fuzzy pink area rug laid over the hardwood floor. Not that she'd been on the floor all night.

Poor Bella had thrown up again, though at least her fever had stayed under 102. She'd tossed and turned and whimpered until Abby finally took her out to the roomy upholstered rocker-recliner in the living room, covered them both with an afghan and held her for a couple hours, rocking slowly. Then she'd finally taken Bella back to bed and hoped for the best.

Between worrying about Bella and wondering

if Jess was all right, each minute had seemed to last an hour. All night long.

"How are you feeling this morning, Bella?"

"My head hurts and I'm cold, then I'm hot. I don't wanna go to school."

"You definitely aren't going to school, honey. And not Sophie either. We need to go to the clinic in town and have them take a look at you both. You might need some medicine to make you feel better."

"Not shots!"

"No shots. I promise." Abby levered herself slowly off the floor and stretched. "I'm going to get dressed and call the clinic, then I'll come back and check on you. Bella, are you hungry at all?"

"Nuh-uh."

"I guessed not, but maybe you'd like some Sprite? We need to keep you hydrated. And Sophie—what about you? Are you ready for some breakfast?"

Sophie already seemed a bit pale, and the suggestion made her color fade even further.

Not a good sign. "I think, ladies, that you should get dressed so we can go to the clinic. I'll be right back."

Betty's door was still closed and Abby could hear her snoring softly, so she went to the kitchen table and called the clinic on her cell, then went back to get dressed and help the girls.

"Your grandma is still asleep, but the clinic nurse says she can fit you in this morning if we hurry."

Her mouth forming a pout, Bella gathered her blankets around her shoulders. "I don't *wanna* go to the doctor."

"I know you don't." Abby pulled matching purple outfits from the closet for the girls. "But if you have the flu and take the right medicine, you might get well quicker. And that's good, isn't it? Then you'll feel like playing with Lollipops and the puppy. And we can finally make those pretty cookies we talked about. Okay?"

The girls nodded and listlessly put on their clothes.

Abby left a note for Betty on the kitchen table, and with a silent prayer and a lot of encouragement she managed to get the girls bundled up, into the SUV and to the clinic before nine o'clock.

The receptionist gave the girls antiviral paper face masks decorated with cartoon pandas and sent them right back to the farthest exam room, where a nurse took their information, checked vitals and promised that the physician's assistant would be in shortly.

Lorena Sanchez, a petite thirtysomething woman with a black ponytail hanging down the middle of her back, arrived with the news Abby feared. Bella's test for influenza was positive, and Sophie's, as well.

"So how are my favorite girls from the Langford ranch?" she said with a cheery smile. "You've probably felt better." She looked up at Abby. "And you are—"

"Abby Halliday, housekeeper. Jess is out of town and Betty can't drive yet."

"It's flu season and I don't shake hands with anyone, but welcome." She turned back to the twins. "Can you both sit up on my table for a minute?"

Their eyes wide and wary, they clambered onto the table and sat still as statues as Lorena completed their exams. She helped them hop off the exam table, offered them a box of stickers to look through, then settled onto the chair in front of a computer screen and began typing.

After a few minutes, she pushed away from the desk and looked at Abby.

"We've had some kiddos come in with flu and the whole shebang—ear infection, sinus infection and the start of pneumonia. But the good news here is that these girls test positive for the flu but haven't developed anything else. And they did have flu shots, so they should end up less sick and get well sooner than most of the folks I see."

She handed an instruction sheet to Abby. "Still, take this home, and be sure to call us if you see any of these changes. It can progress pretty fast—kids might look okay when they're here, but two hours later they need to be admitted to the hospital."

"I'll be very glad when Jess gets back from Denver."

Lorena pursed her lips. "I hope he didn't get caught up in all that bad weather. I saw videos of major pileups on the roads out there on the morning news."

Abby wrapped her arms around her middle, suddenly feeling cold. That was *another* daunting thought.

Come to think of it, why hadn't he called this morning to check on everything at home? She'd texted him and hadn't received a reply. As soon as she was done here, she would try calling. Where was he?

Lorena cocked her head and studied Abby with concern. "How are you and Betty doing? Any symptoms?"

"Not so far… I think."

"I'm sending antiviral prescriptions over to the drugstore so you can drive up to the window and not take the girls inside. It would be a good idea for all of the adults at the ranch to be on it, too, just in case."

Abby nodded.

Lorena went back to her computer and began

typing. "I'm adding prescriptions for Betty and Jess. And you, too, but first the nurse needs to take your health history."

"Of course."

Sophie slumped over and moaned. Lorena darted to the supply cupboard in the corner and dashed back to Sophie with a plastic basin.

"No surprise, there," she said with a sympathetic expression. "I'll just do your health history myself, Abby, to get you on your way faster. I have a feeling it isn't going to be an easy trip home."

By the time Abby gave the girls their first dose of the antiviral medication and settled them in their beds at home, neither protested the thought of taking a nap.

After letting the puppy outside in the fenced yard for a few minutes, she brought him back in and found Betty dozing in her chair by the fireplace.

Betty awoke with a start when the puppy hopped up onto her lap. "Ooof!" she exclaimed, cradling his fluffy golden head between her hands and rubbing behind his ears. "If you'd done that right after my surgery, I would have been on the ceiling. Brrrr. Your little feet are cold and wet!"

"Sorry about that. He slipped by before I could wipe them off," Abby murmured as she dropped onto the sofa facing Betty. "Did you see my note when you got up this morning?"

"I did. How are the girls?"

"Both positive for the flu. Bella had a hard night, and now Sophie is showing symptoms, so they're lying down for a while in their room. The PA gave us all antiviral prescriptions and recommends that everyone here be on it, since the virus is so contagious. And… I'm afraid I can't take you to your rehab appointment. Not with the girls sick."

"No problem." Betty's gnarled hands stilled on the puppy. "Have you heard anything from Jess?"

"Nope. I texted—no answer. And I called, but the phone went right to voice mail."

"I wonder—does he keep a planner in his office?" Betty mused. "Maybe he wrote the name and number of the clients he was going to see on his calendar."

"Good idea."

"Please—go see if you can find out anything." Betty shifted in her chair and winced.

At the doorway of Jess's office Abby hesitated, one hand on the doorframe. Entering this private space seemed intrusive without him here. After a moment, she resolutely strode to his desk. The surface was clean and organized, with a neat stack of mail to the right, some manila folders to the left.

And in the center, a zippered leather planner opened to a two-page November calendar.

Most of the little daily squares were filled with detailed reminders in neat, small handwriting. But for November 12 and 13, Jess had only written *Denver*.

No client name, address or phone number,

She surveyed the room for a wall calendar, but there were just banks of oak bookshelves interspersed with wildlife and horse paintings. Frustrated, she glanced at the planner once more.

Her gaze fell to the week below.

November 16—hired-hand interview 3:00 p.m.

November 20—housekeeper 10:00 a.m.

Housekeeper? She slammed the planner shut, feeling guilty and embarrassed at looking beyond his current Denver trip.

Had he already found someone to take Abby's place? She braced her hands on the desk and took a deep breath. Of course, he needed a permanent employee. That had been clear from the start.

But the thought of never again seeing Betty and the girls—or Jess—made her realize just how much she loved being here. She already cared for them all. And unlike the ranch where she'd grown up, this place felt like *home*.

She'd gotten so caught up in life here at the ranch that she hadn't been focusing on her job search. But if she had to stay up until the wee hours online every night, she was going to double her efforts at searching for another job to tide her over until fall semester.

And no matter where the first decent job was, she needed to be ready to leave.

By nine o'clock on Saturday morning, Abby figured that every mother of young kids deserved a special Mom's Medal of Honor and an annual all-expenses-paid trip to Hawaii.

Both girls had been sick throughout the night, and when they weren't crying, they were whining…though sometimes one would be quiet and lethargic for a while, which was worse. Because then she would suddenly register the silence and launch from her blanket on the floor to hover over that child, filled with worry and doubt.

Their fevers varied but never quite reached 102, which had filled Abby with relief. Still, by three in the morning she was back in the big upholstered rocking chair, this time with both girls snuggled close to her until morning sunshine was streaming through the windows.

Bella stirred and sat up, rubbing her eyes, then looked around. "I feel better," she said in wonder. "Am I still sick?"

Abby rested the back of her hand against Bella's forehead. "Probably for several more days yet, but you seem less feverish. Are you hungry?"

Bella nodded. "Is Sophie sick?"

Still nestled close to Abby's other side, Sophie mumbled something and snuggled even closer. "She feels a bit cooler now, too. This bug can take a week, but between your flu shots and the medicine, I hope you'll soon be on the mend."

Abby shifted and awkwardly reached around Sophie for her cell phone, and checked it for messages.

"Finally," she whispered.

"Finally what?" Bella leaned closer to see the screen.

"Do you see these words? This is a text message from your Uncle Jess. I've been worried about him because he didn't come home last night. But he says he is all right and should be home today. Good news."

Bella perked up. "Maybe he'll bring presents," she breathed. "Sometimes he does, when he goes far away."

"Well…maybe, but I wouldn't count on it. He doesn't say what happened, but I'm guessing he had trouble with bad weather. He might not have been able to get to a store."

Bella threaded her arm through the crook of Abby's elbow and moved closer. "Maybe we could make cookies for when he comes home. Pretty ones, like sparkly ponies."

"Unicorns," Sophie added sleepily as she pulled away and sat up. "I like them best."

"So, Miss Sunshine, how are you feeling? Are you thirsty? I can get you a little water or some Sprite."

Sophie shook her head and lay back down again.

"Well, my dears—it looks like you are having a party out here," Betty said as she pushed her walker into the room. "Can I join you?"

"Please do." Abby searched Betty's face, fearing that she, too, was becoming ill, but her cheeks were rosy and her eyes sparkled. *Thank You, Lord.* "But don't get too close. The girls had a long night, but I think Bella is better. And I finally heard from Jess."

Betty pressed a hand to her chest. "Well, praise be! What did he say?"

"No details—he just texted that he's on his way home."

"Why didn't he call sooner? Can you call him back?"

"I imagine he's driving, and the conditions might still be bad. As much as I want to know what's going on, I just don't want to distract him."

Betty's expression deflated. "Well…just so long as he's not hurt."

Abby gently extricated herself from the twins in

her lap and took Sophie to her bed, then came back. "So, who would like some breakfast? Anybody?"

"Pancakes with chocolate chips?" Bella smiled up at her. "I'm a good helper."

Across the room, Betty's eyes widened and her mouth fell open with surprise.

Abby nodded. "Sounds perfect. Let's go."

She smiled over her shoulder at Betty and shrugged, feeling just as surprised as she was.

If this was the beginning of a better relationship with the little girl, then every sleepless hour had been worth it.

Chapter Fourteen

When Jess arrived back at the ranch at eight o'clock Saturday evening, he could see the girls bouncing excitedly at the window.

If Abby hadn't been standing behind them with her hands on their shoulders, he suspected that they might have run outside in their pajamas to greet him.

Seeing the warm glow of the lights in the house spilling out onto the snow and the people at the window who were eager for him to be home filled him with a sense of connection and sent a rush of warmth through him.

Family.

Oh, Gramma Betty had always been his rock. And the girls had been here almost a year.

But Abby seemed to make the circle complete, and he imagined always returning home to this—a loving woman waiting for him with the children…maybe even more of them—

He caught himself up short.

What was he thinking? She'd left him once before. And she'd already made it clear she was moving on, her heart set on getting her PhD and what she hoped to achieve in autism research. Truly noble goals.

He—and life on this isolated ranch—would never be anything but second best.

He limped to the house, then took a deep breath and forced himself to walk in the door as if he had no injuries at all.

Abby held the girls back until he got his coat and boots off, and then they rushed to him, too excited to hold still. "Just a quick warning—they both tested positive for the flu yesterday, and they probably won't be completely well for three or four days, at the least."

Ignoring the pain knifing through his left shoulder, he scooped them both up anyway, one girl nestled in each arm, and savored the sweet warmth of them when they wrapped their arms around his neck. "I missed you two little punkins," he said with a laugh. "Were you good for your grandma and Abby?"

Bella puffed out her chest. "Abby and me made cookies. Hundreds and thousands."

"You helped?" He lifted an eyebrow in surprise. When he left two days ago, he'd guessed that Bella would rather walk on nails than cooperate with Abby.

"Bella was a super helper. And she did wash her hands very well, I promise," Abby said with a wry smile. "And she didn't handle the cookies after they were baked. But poor Sophie spent most of the day curled up on one of the sofas with the puppy."

He grinned at Bella. "Well, I can't wait to try those cookies, so I'm going to set you girls down."

He gingerly lowered them, steeling himself against the pain running down his left side.

Bella ran over to the counter and pointed to a clear, rectangular container. "They're in boxes 'cause then they'll stay nice. That's what Abby said."

Jess opened the lid. "Wow, these sure are pretty. I bet you used all the sprinkles in the whole county."

She nodded and watched as he took two. "It was Abby's recipe that she made when she was little like me and Sophie."

He wanted to ask about Bella's attitude transformation, but figured he'd better wait. "These are the best cookies ever. Bar none."

Bella beamed at him, then angled a shy smile at Abby. "It was fun."

"I'm gonna help next time," Sophie said wistfully. "If I'm not sick."

"Of course you will." Jess ruffled her long blond curls. "You're a good cookie baker, too."

"The recipe is super easy, especially when you've got good little helpers and need to keep re-rolling the dough. By the way, since the girls are sick, everyone else here should be on antiviral medication." Abby tipped her head toward a white pharmacy bag on the counter. "I picked up some for you, as well. We're all supposed to take it twice a day for five days."

"Thanks." He'd been caught up in the girls' welcome, but now he looked at Abby—really looked at her—and saw the weariness in her face and the dark circles beneath her eyes.

He felt a stab of guilt. "I'm sorry I wasn't here," he said quietly. "You look exhausted."

"It was a long night, but we made it through. Tonight should be better. But I've got to tell you something."

He felt a frisson of alarm. "About…?"

A corner of her mouth twitched. "I did not fully appreciate how much work you were doing here before I came. The house, the meals and the kids are truly a full-time commitment, and how you did the outside work as well I will never know. So… I just wanted to tell you that I am well-and-truly impressed."

He'd feared bad news, but her words were like a gentle balm to his battered body and her gaze, now fixed on his, made his heart give a hard extra thump. He lifted a hand to tuck a wayward lock of her long blond hair behind her ear…

Then he faltered, the intimate mood broken, and scanned the kitchen and the arched doorway into the living room, his concern growing. "Where's Betty? Is she all right?"

The faint blush coloring Abby's cheekbones faded. "She said she wanted to turn in early. She says she feels right as rain and not to worry, but I've still been keeping a close eye on her."

"She's taking the antiviral meds, too, right?"

"Absolutely." Abby opened the refrigerator door and peered inside. "Are you hungry? I can heat up some beef stew if you'd like."

"Thanks, but I grabbed something at a drive-through several hours ago, and I'm all set." He smiled down at Bella and rested a hand on her shoulder. "Especially after Bella's *wonderful* cookies."

Abby glanced at the clock on the stove. "It's bedtime, girls. You got to see Uncle Jess, so now can you each pick out some books for story time? I'll be down to your room in just a minute."

Their faces fell, but both girls were clearly tired and they obediently headed for their bedroom.

"Betty and I were really worried about you. We

tried to call but you didn't answer," Abby said as she sealed up the box of cookies and put it back on the counter. "She even asked me to check your desk to see if you'd written down the name of your client in Denver, but there wasn't a name on your calendar."

The touch of worry in her voice surprised him. "I couldn't call. When you see my truck and trailer, you'll understand why."

She spun around, her eyes wide. "What happened?"

"Glare ice outside Denver. A multivehicle pileup. Semis, SUVs, cars. I was behind the first semi to jackknife and could've avoided it, but cars all around me spun out of control, then a lot more came way too fast. Snow had started falling and hid the ice from the oncoming drivers, I guess."

"We heard about that one on the news," Abby said faintly, her fingertips at her lips as she searched his face. "It sounded awful. You're sure you're all right?"

He nodded, not quite meeting her eyes.

"What about the horses?"

"The truck and the side of the trailer took some pretty good hits on the driver's side, but the horses were fine and the vehicles farther behind us ended up being something of a barricade. We were on the freeway for most of the night waiting while everything got sorted out. But I got the horses delivered, safe and sound."

She blinked. "I'm so sorry to hear you had such trouble. But you're really okay? Honest?"

He shrugged. "A couple of bruises, but nothing important."

"Why didn't you call and let us know? Betty was so worried—and I was, too."

"My phone fell out of my pocket while I was helping an older couple. What with snow starting to fall and random car parts here and there, I didn't find it until someone stepped on the screen."

"But at least you had some food in the trailer kitchen and feed for the horses. Right?"

He nodded. "I ended up with quite a few people in the living quarters, trying to keep warm. Some of those folks were really shook up."

From down the hall came Bella's voice, begging for stories.

"I'd better go," Abby said quietly. She reached out to place her hand on Jess's forearm. "I'm so glad you made it home, Jess."

She hesitated for a moment, as if she wanted to say something more, then turned away and left the kitchen.

After she was gone, he went to the cupboard over the sink and swallowed a couple of ibuprofen tablets. He winced as he raised a water glass to wash them down.

He hadn't wanted Abby's sympathy or, worse, for her to tell Betty—because then there would be a flurry of fussing and questions and worries and hovering.

He would be fine…in a few days. But he had a lot of ranch work to do—work that never ended. And if he didn't find a good man to hire, he could foresee a long, long winter ahead.

Abby stood at the window the next morning and stared out at Jess's truck and trailer. Stunned, she jerked on her jacket and boots and went outside to survey the rig from all sides.

The driver's-side front door and fender had been smashed in, and the rear door on that side was worse. The front bumper had been pried away so it would clear the tire for driving. On the other side there was even more damage. The tack compartment of the trailer had been hit hard enough to buckle and was held shut by wire.

It seemed impossible that Jess could have walked away unscathed. She went back to the driver's-side door and rose on her tiptoes to peer inside. Her stomach lurched.

"Not exactly a new truck anymore, is it?"

She whirled around and found Jess standing behind her. In the early morning sun she now saw bruising on the left side of his jaw.

"There's *blood* in there, Jess. On the inside of

the door and on the steering wheel. You said you weren't hurt." She reached up and gently ran her fingertips under his jaw. "So where did that blood come from?"

He started to shrug. Instantly winced at the obvious pain knifing through his left shoulder. "I've got some bruising down my left side. No broken bones. The second and third impacts hit after the airbags deflated, so my shoulder and ribs are little sore. A few cuts and scrapes…nothing big."

She was now imagining deep, massive bruising the length of his body, future surgery on that shoulder and…

"How many sutures?" she demanded.

He shifted uncomfortably. "Just a dozen. Or so."

"Right. And yet you're out here planning to tackle your chores alone. I'll take over for as long as it takes."

He shook his head. "That isn't necessary."

"I love doing it, and you know it. The girls will be fine with Betty." When he didn't answer, she threw her hands up in exasperation. "Since you had sutures, that means you went to an urgent care or a hospital. What did *they* say about you going right back to work?"

"Nothing."

"Right. And I suppose they didn't say anything about your bruising either. I'd guess your whole left side is already dark black-and-blue." She felt her lips start to tremble and clamped her mouth shut for a moment to regain control.

Jess tilted his head and frowned. "I'm guessing this isn't just about me."

She took a deep breath. "My brother is pig-headed, like some other people I know. He took a bad spill off a bull and had such massive bruising that he ended up with a deep abscess, then infection...and by the time he went to the ER, he was septic. We almost lost him. And that was *before* the accident that put him in a wheelchair."

"Point taken." Jess sighed. "I guess."

"I can't take the girls to church today," Abby continued. "Not while they're sick. So I'm going to check on them and tell Betty I need to be out doing chores."

He looked as if he still wanted to argue, but she gave a firm shake of her head. "You can put your feet up in the tack room or go up to the house. But at least for today, you're not doing a thing."

Chapter Fifteen

True to her word, Abby took over the outside chores starting Sunday and harassed Jess if he tried to do too much. But on Tuesday afternoon he felt better, and the prospective ranch hand he'd talked to last week actually came on time for an interview.

Jess had already done a background check on him, so when Phil Crandall showed up with a reference in hand from a big cattle operation in Texas and gave knowledgeable answers to every question Jess asked, it didn't take long to decide.

While Phil waited in the kitchen with a cup of coffee, Jess went back to his office to follow up on the man's reference letter with a phone call, then hired him on the spot.

"Phil's cabin is all set," Abby said at breakfast the next morning. "I scrubbed everything and took a set of bed linens and towels up there. It's a nice little place, actually. Have you ever rented out those cabins to tourists?"

Jess shook his head. "Dad built just three of them to house a foreman and several hired hands, but we've only had one ranch hand at a time here during the past few years."

"They're nice enough for tourists, if you ever decide to run a dude ranch." She winked at him. "I'm sure you'd love that. Kids running everywhere, petting the cows and horses...exploring the tack room, climbing on the hay bales."

He knew she was teasing, but he still cringed at the thought. "Strangers in and out of here all the time? Dealing with that kind of liability on a working ranch? No thanks."

Betty looked up from her crossword puzzle. "I always thought it might be fun, meeting all of those people from who knows where, but your dad never wanted to rent the cabins either."

Abby started clearing the table. "So how do I handle a hired hand's meals and laundry?"

"There's a laundry room in the tack room, where we wash the horse blankets." Jess took a sip of coffee. "He can use those machines or go to the laundromat in town."

He went to pull on his boots and jacket. "As for meals, the hired hands usually join us, but this guy seemed pretty noncommittal. I'll ask him what he prefers so you'll know what to expect."

At the sound of an old pickup rattling up the lane, Poofy started barking and the twins left the table to peek out the kitchen windows.

Bella looked at Jess over her shoulder. "He has a funny truck. It's different colors."

Jess looked out the window. "It looks like he's replacing the fenders and doors piece by piece as he can afford to. When it's done he'll probably paint it all one color."

"Now it's like a coat of many colors, girls." Betty set aside her pencil and closed her book of puzzles. "Do you remember the Bible story about Joseph?"

Bella nodded. "His coat must have been pretty."

"Sophie is staying home sick another day, so we'll hear that story again when you get home, Bella," Abby said. "But we need to get to the school bus in less than ten minutes, so go brush your teeth and put on your coat and boots. Quickly."

Quickly was a subjective word, Jess had discovered, when it came to getting the girls off to school. Even if he'd collected boots, shoes, hats, mittens and backpacks the night before, it was always a scramble in the morning. Especially when the girls weren't cooperative.

"Bella, I need to go outside to welcome the new ranch hand. But I want to see you bundled up and heading for the bus stop in *eight* minutes, all right? No excuses."

Bella raced down the hall to the bathroom, and Abby looked up from stuffing papers into her backpack to give him an amused smile. "I guess I need to practice my Jess voice."

Her smile made his insides tighten and made him want to linger just to see it again. He wondered if there was any way that she could be as aware of him as he was of her.

But he doubted it.

She was the one who had left town, married someone else and been gone for twelve long years. He needed to ignore the old feelings that kept resurfacing and just move on.

But with every passing day that was getting harder to do.

Abbie left Sophie in the house with Grandma Betty, and after putting Bella on the school bus, she went looking for Jess and his new hired hand. She found them in the feed room of the horse barn, where Jess was pointing out the complex, individualized rations listed on a blackboard for the thirty horses in the barn.

He glanced at her. "Abby Halliday, this is Phil Crandall. Phil, Abby is our nanny."

The new hired hand was wiry, maybe five foot six, wearing faded jeans, scuffed roper boots and a fleece-lined denim jacket. Beneath his crumpled Stetson she could see that his weather-beaten, leathery skin spoke of a lifetime spent in the Montana sun.

He pointedly studied her bare left hand, then glanced between Jess and her as if sizing up the situation. Then he fixed his eyes on hers and bared his tobacco-stained teeth in a semblance of a smile. "Very nice making your acquaintance, ma'am. The scenery just got a whole lot nicer on this winter day."

Relief slid through her when he didn't extend a hand to her, but even so she took a step back. "I'm sure you'll be a great help around here, Mr. Crandall."

Jess slanted a curious look at her. "Phil and I were just talking. He says he'd rather not come up to the house for breakfast and lunch, but he'll join us for dinner."

Phil chuckled, his gaze still riveted on Abby. "You know, I've just had second thoughts about lunch. Good food, good company, nice scenery… how could I pass that up?"

"Right." She felt a cold shiver race through her. "Jess, I need to take Betty to her PT appointment after lunch. Will you be able to watch Sophie?"

Jess nodded. "I'll stay in the house with her until you get back."

"You'll watch her closely, right? She's still not feeling well. The digital thermometer is in the—"

"Medicine cabinet, top shelf," Jess said dryly. "I won't leave her for a minute. This isn't my first rodeo with the girls being sick, you know. Betty and I have dealt with strep throat, norovirus, ear aches and bronchitis. Not at the same time, of course."

She felt her cheeks flush. It was true. She'd been here for two weeks, but Jess had been responsible for the girls for almost a year. What was she thinking? Except…with every day she spent with them, she loved them more, and it was already hard to leave them in someone else's care.

"Of course—you're right," she said, a little embarrassed. "It's just…"

"I know. While I'm in the house with Sophie, Phil can finish settling into his cabin, then he can start hauling hay out to the cattle." He shot a quick grin at his new hired hand. "Great having you on board."

He turned back to the blackboard to continue discussing horse feed and Abby hurried to the house, feeling as if spiders had just skittered down her back.

She knew Jess had done a background check on Phil. The man hadn't said anything blatantly wrong and he hadn't made a wrong move. Yet something about him warned her of danger, and she'd learned long ago to listen to her instincts.

She silently reviewed the techniques she learned in the self-defense classes she'd taken while teaching in Chicago's inner-city schools.

She just hoped she wouldn't need them.

After serving lunch, and carefully avoiding eye contact with Phil, who seemed to watch her every move, Abby watched him head for his cabin, then left Sophie and Jess playing a round of Candy Land by the fireplace and took Betty into town for her PT appointment.

In the parking lot of the clinic, she helped Betty get started with her walker and went with her to the front desk. As soon as she was checked in, Abby helped her take a seat in the waiting room. "You certainly seem more stable on your feet now. And a lot more chipper, as well."

"With all of the exercises I'm doing, I should be ready for the next Winter Olympics," Betty said with a chuckle. "Either ice dancing or the luge. What do you think?"

Abby laughed and gave her wrinkled hand a gentle, affectionate squeeze. "I wouldn't put either of them past you. I'm going to run a few errands. Call me if you're done early, but otherwise I'll be back at the usual time."

Abby stepped out of the clinic into the bright

winter sunshine and headed down the sidewalk to Millie's Café, wondering if her father would actually show up.

The chances were probably slim to none if Darla had seen Abby's text this morning, so she might end up sitting alone with her cup of coffee back at the rehab clinic. But she had to try.

Inside the front door, she scanned the coffee shop with its old-fashioned lunch counter, where two retired ranchers were hunched over their coffees talking cattle prices, then glanced around the dining area. A dozen empty Formica-topped tables filled the center space, while six booths with high backs lined up along the big front windows.

Defeated, she turned to leave, when she saw her father stand up slowly from the farthest booth.

He rolled the brim of his old Resistol in both hands—a nervous gesture that touched her heart because he'd raised her to follow his rule that no real cowboy ever risked damaging the perfect curve of his hat brim.

"Hey, Dad," she said softly. "I'm glad you came."

He nodded once and waved her into the booth, then lifted his coffee mug and gestured to the waitress behind the counter.

The woman brought a cup of coffee over for Abby. "Anything else, darlin'?"

"Do you still serve Millie's strawberry-rhubarb pie?"

"Sure enough—and she still makes it herself, every day. There's just one slice left, if you want it."

"Yes, ma'am. For my dad. À la mode, please."

The waitress nodded and returned with the pie, then disappeared into the kitchen.

"Do you remember this, Dad?"

He forked up a bite of the delectable ruby pie filling and flaky crust. "You always wanted this whenever you came into town with me. When you were just a little girl."

"Now you'll get to set new traditions with Lanna, right?" Abby asked gently, watching his expression. "Now that you've married her mother."

"I should have told you about Darla. But everything just happened so fast." He dropped his gaze to the plate in front of him. "And she's been real afraid."

"Why?" Abby asked cautiously.

"I think she thought you'd try to talk some sense into me before it was too late," he admitted gruffly. "You get to my age and figure you'll just have another decade alone, and then you'll die."

"Oh, Dad," Abby whispered. "That sounds so sad."

He shrugged. "It is what it is. But then someone with a loving heart comes along, and how can you turn away from that?"

"Where did you two meet?"

"An Angus-cattle convention. Reno."

"She's a *rancher*?"

"Does she look like a rancher to you, with all that glitter?" His laugh lines deepened briefly, as if he were recalling a sweet memory. "She was a hostess in the convention hall. It was crowded, and she bumped into me with an armload of catalogs. They flew all over the floor. And then she started to cry."

"You would have told me to just pick it all up, stop sniveling and get back to work."

The depth of sadness in his eyes nearly stole her breath. "After your mom left I made so many mistakes with you, Abby. But it's too late to change anything now."

He'd been cold and stern, and he'd often dealt with conflicts by stomping out of the house and disappearing into the barn, leaving her confused and angry and even a little afraid. She'd cried herself to sleep many a time as a child. Yeah, there'd been mistakes—but then she hadn't been perfect either.

"I always figured I could've done better at raising a boy. But when you came along all pretty and sweet, I was buffaloed from day one. Never did know how to say or do the right thing with any woman—but especially with you. Never had the patience either."

Hearing his voice break as he laid bare those

regrets chipped at the wall she'd built around her heart. She was an adult now, not an emotional teenager perpetually hurt and angry at his distant demeanor. It was time to let go of the past.

"Parents try to do their best, Dad. No one is born an expert."

"The one thing I knew was that the world was a hard place for a woman. Unforgiving. Dangerous. So I tried to make you tough, so nothing could ever break you. But maybe all I ever did was drive you away." His brow furrowed. "Now I have a chance to do better, and I'm hoping I don't mess this up, too."

"With Lanna?"

"Darla." He lifted his gaze from his coffee. "That day she and I met? She was overwhelmed after a fight with her ex-husband. Terrified that he might keep her from seeing her daughter. Darla happened to fall apart right in front of me, and for once in my life, I must've said the right things. We went for coffee and talked for hours. *Me.*" He shook his head in wonder. "I figured she was way too young for an old coot like me. But, well…"

"You ended up together," Abby said gently.

He'd always been cantankerous. Impatient. But now he seemed…more at peace, somehow.

"Now I just hope I can make her happy. She's never had a real family—the kind that sticks with you no matter what. Wrong side of the tracks, some scrapes with the law in high school. Always ended up with the wrong guys."

"She had a rough life."

"She never had much until she married Greg, and then she found out money isn't everything. He turned out to be a big mistake. We had to change the house phone and cell numbers because he called all times of the day and night harassing her. I finally did give him the ranch number again because of Lanna, but told him we'd block him if he caused any more trouble."

Abby shuddered. "What if he comes to your ranch?"

"He does sometimes, to drop off Lanna. But the first time he tried to harass Darla, I marched him back out to his shiny new Navigator with my shotgun." Dad snickered. "I said he was welcome to pick up or drop off their daughter. But if he tried to intimidate Darla again, I would report him to the sheriff and those fancy tires and the side of that SUV would be full of buckshot. And he would be next."

"What did he do, threaten you right back?"

Dad snorted. "That rich, spoiled city boy? He's the kind who enjoys bullying someone weaker but is terrified of facing the same thing himself."

He pushed his coffee mug to one side. "I don't judge Darla for the choices she made in her past, and she doesn't care that I'm older—that I'm not some guy with a fancy job and flashy car. We're a good, solid match, honey."

Honey? He'd never called her that. If Darla's influence softened this much, it was a miracle. A warm glow filled her heart. "One of the little Langford twins thought Darla was pretty as a princess."

"I figured she always wore flashy clothes to feel better about herself." His smile faded. "I hoped things would be better for her once we were hitched. But she says people in town look down at her as if she were a gold digger who caught herself a lonely old man. It breaks her heart. Betty is the only person in town who even welcomed her."

Abby felt a niggle of guilt over her own assumptions, though Darla had hardly been friendly either. "Maybe everyone just needs to get to know her better."

He glanced around the empty coffee shop, then lowered his voice. "It's nobody's business but ours. But people are dead wrong if they think she came after my money. She knows that almost everything I own is in a revocable trust with only your name on it, and that's how it will stay."

Abby blinked. "I never meant to pry. I mean, I didn't—"

He waved away her rising embarrassment. "I set it all up with my lawyer years ago. But just so you know, I did update my will. When I die,

Darla will be able to buy a nice house somewhere and will have some money to live on. I figure it's only fair."

"Of course, Dad. But honestly, I hadn't thought about all of this," Abby said faintly. "I've never imagined a time when you wouldn't be out on the ranch raising your Angus cattle."

"If you fail to set up a will, you're a fool. You'll leave a big, expensive legal mess for your family," he growled. "That's what my father said to me, and it's what I'm telling you."

"Yes, sir."

Dad reached across the table and rested his hand on hers. "It's been a long time, Abby. I'm glad you're back."

"Me, too. I hope we can stay in touch after I leave." Her gaze fell on his work-worn hand, the thinning flesh revealing the intricate outlines of the bones and rope-like veins, and she thought about how hard he'd worked all his life.

If Darla made him happy and she treated him right, then that was all Abby needed to know.

She caught a glimpse of his watch. "Oh my word! I need to pick up Betty Foster at the clinic. She's waiting for me."

She slipped on her jacket and gathered her purse and gloves. "I... I hope you and Darla will be very happy, Dad. Maybe we can all get together sometime? Though I'm not sure Darla would like that."

Rising to his feet, Dad pulled on his coat and settled his old Resistol in place. "I know how she's been toward you since you came back to town, and we had a long talk. She's scared that you'll do everything you can to talk me into believing that our marriage was a mistake."

"She must think I'm an ogre," Abby said with a pained laugh.

"No—just a grown-up daughter who's worried about her father."

"To be honest, I *was* concerned. If she was trying to take advantage of you, I would do everything I could to protect you. But…it sounds like everything is going to be okay."

"Maybe for you, too," he said as he pulled on his gloves. He raised an eyebrow. "Could be you'll decide to stick around."

"If you're referring to Jess, there's no chance of that." At the door of the café, she stopped. "You know, Thanksgiving is next week. Would you two like to join us for dinner?"

His eyes lit up. "That would be real nice. I'll need to ask Darla. I'm hoping she says *yes*."

"Me, too, Dad." And as Abby walked out the door, she was surprised at how much she really meant it.

Chapter Sixteen

On Sunday morning Jess walked beside Betty as they headed for the ramp to the right of the main church entrance, his hand hovering at her elbow.

With the temps hovering in the 40s and bright sunshine, the heavy snowdrifts had melted down to small mounds of slush and the sidewalks were bare, but with a brisk wind blowing from the north, none of the other parishioners were gathered outside to talk.

He helped Betty through the door and smiled as she made a beeline for a group of her friends chattering to one side.

"Howdy, Jess." Pastor Bob clapped a hand on Jess's back. He lowered his voice. "Any more word from California?"

The noise level in the entryway increased as a flood of children poured from the Sunday-school wing and scattered, looking for their parents.

Surveying the entryway to make sure the twins weren't close enough to overhear, Jess shook his head. "Just Lindsey's phone call, but it was over two weeks ago. I have no idea if she'll actually show up, so I'm not saying anything to the girls."

"Good. Poor little lambs. No sense getting their hopes up." Bob rubbed his snowy beard. "But at least you know their mom is still living."

Jess nodded his head, then turned and saw Abby appear in the doorway, holding each of the twins by the hand. Her silky crimson blouse shimmered, clinging to every slender curve.

Apparently he wasn't the only one who noticed her, because Trace Jorgensen, the local banker, took one look and headed straight toward her with a wolfish smile on his face.

Jess ground his teeth and forced his attention back to the pastor. "Sorry, Pastor, what did you say?"

Bob gave him a knowing smile. "I shouldn't keep you from your family, and I see someone I need to talk to. Take care."

But before Jess could reach Abby and the twins, Maura stepped in his path and brushed a swift kiss against his cheek. "How's everything out at the ranch?"

Jess dragged his attention from Abby to the woman now standing squarely in his way. "Fine."

She glanced over her shoulder at Abby, then

rested a hand on his arm. "I left you a message but haven't heard back. Have you thought about redecorating your office yet?"

He frowned. "Redecorating?"

"Your *office*."

"Uh, no. Maybe someday."

Her face fell for just a moment; then she rallied, and her determined smile returned. "Well, you do remember the Christmas-program rehearsals are coming up after Thanksgiving, right?"

He blinked. "Rehearsals?"

"For all the children. I've scheduled them for the first, second and third Sundays in December. Since this is your first time through all of this with children, I thought you might need a little reminder." She pressed a folded sheet of paper into his hand and smiled up at him. "We handed these out last Sunday, but your girls weren't here. They *will* be part of the Christmas program, right?"

He started to say, *Yes, if they're still here in Montana*, but caught himself just in time. Mentioning that uncertainty to one of the local busybodies would lead to a conversation he didn't want to pursue, and then see it shared with everyone in town.

He looked over her shoulder and caught Abby's gaze drift between him and Maura. She gave him a faint smile, then turned back to Trace.

Maura gave his arm a flirtatious little shake. "Jess?"

The temptation to brush her aside and interrupt Trace's obvious interest in Abby caught him by surprise.

There were a dozen reasons why he had no right to feel possessive, and just as many reasons why he and Abby would never again be involved. This surge of protectiveness had no place in their business relationship. But still...

He jerked his thoughts back to the woman standing in front of him and tried to remember what she'd just said. "Uh...yes. Thanks. They'll be here for the Christmas program."

"You seem mighty distracted today, cowboy." Maura move a little closer. "I miss you. Maybe we can get together again just for old times' sake? And if there's ever any way I can be of extra help with your sweet little girls..."

This time he looked at her—really looked—and saw the hope in her eyes mingled with a touch of jealousy and desperation. Because of Abby? But he and Maura had been down this road before and it had always ended up the same. Her blatant disinterest in the twins had been the final straw.

And having Abby in his life again—for whatever brief time it would be—had made him see that no one else would ever take her place.

A woman in high heels instead of Western boots would never be the right fit for his life.

"I'm sorry, Maura. Excuse me." He took a step around her and headed toward Abby and the girls. "So how was Sunday School?"

Sophie looked up at him. "We got a cupcake. And juice."

"And pages to color," Bella added. "And we heard a story about Baby Jesus coming soon. It was fun."

"Good. I'm glad." He gave Trace a long, level look. "How are things with your wife and kids?"

"Fine, fine…" The other man glanced between Jess and Abby, then backed away. "Excuse me. I suppose I'd better round them up before the service starts."

Abby choked back a laugh. "Did you just intimidate that man somehow?"

Jess shrugged. "What did I say?"

She rolled her eyes. "Funny, but I thought I just saw a death glare, though I'm not sure why. He was only telling me an amusing story about Pine Bend. Anyway, it looked like you and Maura were having a nice conversation. I didn't want to interrupt."

"Like Trace just said, he's a family man. But he still has an eye for any pretty lady who crosses his path…just so you know."

"And I think Maura still has an eye for you," Abby teased lightly. "If I'm not mistaken."

"She's a good person and deserves to find the right man someday," Jess said in a low voice so no one else would hear. "Though that guy just isn't me. I think she knows it and is just too stubborn to admit it."

The initial notes of "Beautiful Savior" drifted from the sanctuary and the few stragglers chatting in the entryway started heading to the pews.

Jess ushered the twins and Abby to the usual Langford spot on the left, halfway down, where Betty had already taken a seat.

They'd missed church last Sunday because the girls were ill, and the weekend before they had been snowed in, so few of these folks had seen Abby around town. Now, from the corner of his eye, he saw the curious glances and heard whispers travel through the pews.

Some of them might've known her family and maybe even recognized her from years ago, while others were too new to the area. But—typical small town—everyone seemed to find her arrival fascinating.

He didn't blame them a bit.

With that cascade of wavy blond hair and her shimmering blouse, she looked as out of place as a pretty little Arabian filly in a pen of Brahman bulls.

Bella and Sophie usually sat on either side of Betty during church services. But today they were nestled close to Abby's sides.

How she'd won them over he wasn't sure, but the maternal way she curved her arms around them to draw them closer captivated him...

And also made him think about his worries.

He hadn't heard anything more from Lindsey, and he had no way of contacting her. *Before Christmas*, she'd said. Was she already on her way to Montana? Had she changed her mind? Or did she plan to swoop into town and whisk the twins back to California over the holidays? And why didn't she call to let him know her current plans?

He forced his gaze to the front of the church when Pastor Bob began his sermon on prayer, wishing his own prayers could be answered. Wishing he knew *what* to ask for.

Pastor Bob's voice rang through the church with power and conviction, drawing Jess's attention back to the sermon. "...from Philippians Chapter Four, we read '...in everything by prayer and supplication with thanksgiving let your requests be made known unto God. And the peace of God, which passeth all understanding, shall keep your hearts and minds through Christ Jesus.'"

Jess closed his eyes. Offered up a prayer for the best possible future for Lindsey and her girls—whatever that might be.

And then prayed that God was listening.

* * *

Walking into the Pine Bend Community Church was like stepping back in time, Abby thought as the sermon ended.

The soaring white steeple still stood tall and determined against the wild, powerful forces of nature with the mountains close by.

The dozen stained-glass windows had always been Abby's favorite part of this beautiful building. As a child, she'd loved to gaze at the brilliant colors and Bible scenes each one depicted.

Savoring the warmth of the little girls snuggled against her, she breathed in the scents of the candles on the altar and the matching bouquets on either side. The fragrance of those lilies, roses and carnations brought back a flood of memories from her youth. Funerals. The day of her confirmation. The weddings of relatives and family friends, with her always sitting between her parents.

At least until Mom had abruptly decided she'd had it with Dad, ranch life and Montana and taken off for Omaha.

With a start, Abby realized that everyone was standing up to leave.

A frown furrowed Sophie's forehead as she stared at something on the other side of the sanctuary, then pointed. "Abby! It's the sparkly lady. See?"

"Shhhh, Sophie. Not so loud," Abby whispered. "We need to be polite."

"But—"

Abby turned to discreetly look in the direction the child was pointing and found her gaze colliding with Darla's. Even from across the room, it was obvious that the poor woman had overheard Sophie. Her cheeks were bright red, and she looked mortified. Abby's father was nowhere in sight.

Abby looked over her shoulder at Betty. "Can you keep an eye on the girls? I need to do some damage control before it's too late."

Darla quickly gathered her silver coat and matching bag and headed down the far aisle, her head down. Abby skirted the crowd and caught up with her just before she slipped out a side door.

"Darla—please wait."

Darla pulled open the door to leave but stopped when Abby touched her arm. "What do you want?"

"I—I'm so glad to see you. I've been hoping I'd have a chance to chat with you sometime, and here you are."

There were still bright flags of color on Darla's cheekbones, and she lifted her chin with a touch of defiance in her eyes. "Well?"

"I've been working at the Langfords' ranch, and I'm not sure if you heard one of the little girls speak too loudly a few minutes ago, but she adores your beautiful coat. I think it's beautiful, too, but I just hope you weren't offended by her remark."

The defiance in Darla's eyes didn't waver. "I hear you talked to Don last week."

"I've missed my dad, Darla. I wasn't able to get back here for several years because my husband was ill, and I've wanted to make up for lost time." Abby hesitated, searching for the right words. "When I heard he'd suddenly gone off to Vegas to get married, I'll admit I was worried. It didn't sound like the Dad I knew."

Darla froze, and in that moment she seemed like something made of spun glass that could shatter at the slightest touch. "I know what people think." Her brittle voice was cold as ice. "I see them giving me the side-eye when I pass. And I hear what they all say about me. I'm not stupid."

Please, Lord, help me get this right.

"I'm not judging you, Darla. Or my dad. I have no right to do that. And no one else does either." Abby took a deep breath. "He told me that things haven't always been easy in your life. And he said that until you came along, he figured he'd be alone and lonely until he died. I think you've brought him a lot of happiness. And if you're both happy, that's what counts."

Darla didn't answer, but her hard mask seemed to slip a little, and in that moment Abby's heart ached for the lonely, vulnerable woman she glimpsed inside.

Abby heard the thunder of little feet behind her and bit back a smile as the girls reached her and tugged on her coat.

"Uncle Jess and Gramma are in the car, Abby. Waiting right outside."

Abby rested her hands on their shoulders. "The twins are Bella and Sophie, and I have the great pleasure of taking care of them. Girls, can you say hi to Mrs. Peterson? She's newly married to my father."

The girls mumbled a greeting, then raced back to the main door of the church. "Sorry about that. And now I suppose I'd better catch up before I get left behind."

Darla nodded.

"Dad did ask you about Thanksgiving, right? I'd love if you two could come. We'd have a lot more time to visit, and you wouldn't have to make Thanksgiving dinner for just two—or three, if your daughter is with you. She's welcome, too."

Darla hesitated, then shook her head. "I don't think so. That's your family."

"Well, it's not my family either—I'm just the hired help. And it's not going to be a crowd. Just the four Langfords, a ranch hand and me. That's only six, so it would be great to have two more. Please?"

Darla's expression wavered, then her mouth hardened. "No. Thanks all the same."

"The people around here haven't had a chance to get to know you, but I think Betty and I can change that. Things could be different for you here, I promise."

Darla gave a single shake of her head, but as she turned to go, Abby thought she saw a tear start to fall down her cheek.

Abby looked back to the altar, then lifted her gaze to the beautiful stained-glass window above it, which depicted Jesus and his lambs. *Lord, I think I was meant to see her here today. I know she's hurting. I promise You, I won't give up on her... and I'm going to make things right before I leave.*

Chapter Seventeen

On Monday afternoon the temperature was even warmer than the day before, and felt like a bit of spring, though Abby wasn't fooled. With Thanksgiving just a few days away there were a lot of winter months ahead, and she'd seen blizzards hitting as late as April.

She finished saddling Lollipops and studied the haphazard braids the girls were attempting with his thick white mane. "You two are doing a fine job," she announced. "And this is one very patient pony. Do you think he likes being pretty?"

"He's sure not as pretty as you." Phil stopped so close to her that she could smell the tobacco on his breath and see the red capillaries in his eyes.

A shudder rolled down her spine.

The sensual slide to Phil's Southern drawl was absent if Jess was near, and always just subtle enough that it could almost be missed, but she heard it loud and clear. Every single time.

He'd been here seven days now. He hadn't made a single inappropriate, physical move. Yet he always seemed to invade her space and even the simplest words out of his mouth sounded suggestive, somehow.

But as much as his frequent, looming presence bothered her, what could she say to Jess? That the man stood a little too close? That he complimented her?

Alan had never believed her when she'd had trouble with a principal at school, and that man had been far more blatant. She could hardly expect Jess to fire Phil over something so trivial—not when his help was so badly needed. Whatever else she thought about him, Phil was a hard worker. Already Jess seemed less stressed at the end of each day.

"We'll get out of your way," she said stiffly as she unsnapped the cross ties, slipped off Lollipops's halter and bridled him. "Come on, girls."

"I'll be happy to help you out anytime, ma'am," he called out after her. "You just say the word."

Abby herded the girls down the aisle ahead of her and led the pony into the indoor arena. "It's Sophie's turn to go first, Bella. Do you want to see if you can find the kittens in the hay?"

The heated building was a hundred by two-hundred feet, with the actual working arena fenced off to allow for two risers of bleachers along one side, space at one end for hay storage and a path around the entire arena for foot traffic.

Bella ran over to the hay and several calico kittens promptly popped out of their hiding places between the bales to greet her.

Keeping one eye on her, Abby led Sophie around the arena twice. "Are you ready to go by yourself?"

Sophie nodded, her expression serious.

Abby unhooked the lead rope and handed her the reins. "Remember, he's lazy."

Sophie wiggled her boots against his wooly winter coat, nudging him with her heels.

"Harder, Sophie. You can do it!"

"I think I like petting better than riding," she said with a glum voice. "He doesn't want to go."

Abby took hold of Lollipops's reins by the bit and tugged until he started walking forward, then she backed away. "Remember, keep him going," she called out. "Thatta girl!"

Lollipops made it halfway around the arena before stopping by the gate—where he apparently assumed he could leave and go back to his stall. Abby ran over to help get him going again, then stayed by the gate for the next go-round when the pony would surely try that ploy once again.

"There you go, sweetie. You're doing great!"

Sophie cast a proud, shy smile at Abby, then concentrated on making the pony walk. When they approached the gate the next time around she thumped him harder with her heels, and Lollipops broke into a trot for a few strides.

Sophie giggled. "He's a good boy today," she cried. "I made him run!"

Abby smothered a smile as she thumped her palm on the pony's fluffy rear end to keep him going. "That was a trot, and you did a super good job at it. Uncle Jess will be so proud."

After another fifteen minutes Bella had her turn, and Lollipops clearly sensed a more dominant rider on his back because he didn't try to stop and he even trotted all the way around the arena. Once.

Abby leaned against the fence and watched her progress. Behind her, she heard the sliding door open and even without turning, she sensed that it was Jess. "The girls are doing very well, though I see what you mean about looking for a different pony."

Jess came up beside her and hooked one of his boots on the lowest bar of the pipe fence, then braced his hands on the top bar to watch Bella. "I'm glad you're getting the girls out here to ride after school. Do you think they'll remember this if they move away?"

She heard a slight catch in his voice. "I think

they would remember a lot. What little girl doesn't dream of having horses and ponies? Just take lots of pictures and send them home with albums of their life here. They won't forget. But you don't know for sure that they're leaving. Right?"

He turned to look at her. "I can't stop watching the days tick by and wondering if Lindsey is going to show up or not. If she does, I hope she'll be willing to at least let them come for visits over the summer. Holidays. Any time she'd be willing to send them or even come along."

"I hope so, too."

"And what about you?"

"Me?"

"If you're in graduate school next year, could you come back for the summer?" he teased. "I promise I'll have enough ponies for everyone."

"That entirely depends on the pony." She gave him a playful nudge with her shoulder and tipped her head toward Lollipops, who was now at a dead stop in the center of the arena. "I guess I'd rather have your horse. Bart."

They turned back to watching Bella, who finally got the pony moving again. Jess draped his arm casually across Abby's shoulders, just as he had years ago. "It's a good life out here. Do you ever miss it?"

The warmth of his arm around her seemed to

rocket straight to her heart, and it took a while to find her voice.

Longer, to find the right words.

She'd missed him for years after she left Montana, especially after she and Alan drifted apart. "Ranch country is in my blood, and seeing the Rockies on the horizon every day feels like home. I missed that while I was in Chicago. Very much."

It felt so right, standing so close to Jess with his arm around her. It felt like the old days and like new possibilities, and she could no longer deny to herself that maybe she'd never really fallen out of love with him.

But she'd seen him with Maura at church yesterday. Her light kiss. The intimate way she'd held his arm. Jess was the most honest man Abby had ever known, and she believed him when he said that relationship was over. But it sure hadn't looked like Maura thought so.

So whether Abby was falling in love with Jess again or had never stopped, it didn't really matter. Maura would be around long after Abby had to leave, and the woman clearly didn't plan to give up.

Abby pulled the heavy cast-iron Dutch oven out of the oven and settled it on a hot pad. The aroma of roasted chicken wafted into the room when she lifted the lid to check on it.

Satisfied, she put the lid back on and slid a pan of homemade cheddar biscuits into the oven. Then looked over at Betty, who was placing romaine lettuce in the salad spinner. "I'm impressed, Betty. You're doing really well with your new cane."

"About time," Betty grumbled. "This morning I told the physical therapist that the walker was getting in my way, and she finally gave in. How could I help you with Thanksgiving dinner pushing that contraption around?"

"About Thanksgiving," Abby said with a warning look, "I don't want you to work too hard."

Betty frowned. "I've been making Thanksgiving dinner since I was in high school, and I'm not stopping now."

"No—of course not. But there's two of us cooking this year, and I thought we could start some of the food Wednesday, so it wouldn't be such a last-minute rush for either of us."

"How are we going to do that and still have everything fresh and tasty?"

"Maybe do the pies and cranberry sauce? We could even make and freeze our dinner rolls."

"Hmm." Betty took a quick survey of the kitchen. "I'll go call the girls for supper. By the way—I saw your dad and his wife at the clinic, and he said to count on them for Thanksgiving. His wife looked like she'd just eaten a whole dill pickle when he said it, though."

"Then there's hope, anyway. Good."

Abby glanced at the back door, expecting Phil to show up any minute. Tonight Jess had gone to a cattleman's-association meeting in town, and he wouldn't be home until after the girls' bedtime, adding to Abby's usual sense of unease around Phil.

Still, she always had her cell phone. She could handle herself well, should the need arise. And if there was any actual trouble, she wouldn't hesitate about letting Jess know.

Betty herded the girls to the table just as Abby was taking the biscuits out of the oven.

Sophie's eyes opened wide when Abby carved the chicken and arranged it on a large platter framed by the veggies. "That looks yummy! Can I have a drumstick?"

"Of course. And Bella can have the other one, if she'd like."

Phil came in the back door just as they were saying grace. He kicked off his boots and dumped his jacket by the door, then sauntered over to the table. He'd put on a clean shirt and his thin black hair had been slicked back.

Instead of taking his usual chair, he settled where Jess always sat. "I guess the boss isn't here tonight, so I get to sit next to these pretty little ladies." He looked at Bella and Sophie a little too long, his mouth pulled back into a faint smile. "He can't have all the fun now, can he?"

Abby met Betty's gaze and saw that the concern in the older woman's eyes echoed her own.

Phil had been subtle until now. He'd made no overt move, had said nothing that was over the edge. But now...had Jess's absence unleashed his darker side?

She passed the serving platter of chicken to him, followed by the mashed potatoes, broccoli and the basket of hot rolls.

She tried to eat her dinner, but it was as if everything had turned to sawdust. Finally she set her fork aside and dredged up a smile. "So, Bella and Sophie—what was the very best part of your day at school?"

"Story time," Sophie said in a quiet voice. "On the carpet. It was a story about elephant babies."

"What about you, Bella?"

"I liked our visitor best. He was a policeman, and he told us about his job."

"He was probably the sheriff or a deputy, Bella. That's what we have in this county. Did he say what he liked best?"

"Helping people. He does it every day."

"Throws them in jail, more like it." Phil laughed harshly. "And then throws away the key so they have to stay there and rot forever."

Her eyes wide, Bella shot a furtive glance at

him and then looked at Abby. "But the policeman said he likes to *help* people. Did he tell a lie?"

"Of course not, honey. Phil was just making a joke, and it wasn't very funny." She gave Phil a pointed look. "Now, maybe we should all just eat our dinners. Okay?"

He snickered under his breath. "Yes, ma'am."

When everyone was finished, Abby cleared the table and brought out still-warm homemade chocolate puddings for everyone.

Phil idly twirled his spoon through his dessert, dawdling. He got up to get a coffee refill and sat down again, clearly in no hurry to leave.

Betty frowned at him, then Abby. "I'm taking the girls to their room to get them ready for bed. If you need any help out here, just holler."

Abby cleared the rest of table and began loading the dishwasher. She could feel Phil's eyes on her, watching every move as she sealed the leftovers in containers.

She'd tried to be open and fair. She'd tried not to be judgmental. But he'd crossed the line when he leered at the girls at dinner. She felt her anger rise, along with a powerful surge of protectiveness, and if she did nothing else at this ranch, she was going to make sure he left before anything worse happened.

"Are you done yet, Phil?"

Again, that leering smile. "Oh, you bet."

He sat back in his chair and stretched out his legs as if settling in for a good long while, his gaze riveted on her chest. "You can take everything away."

She would *not* be leaning over to take those dishes in front of him, not while he was still there. *Waiting.* "Dinner is over. It's time for you to head back to your cabin, Phil."

He made no move to get up from his chair. "You seem awfully jumpy, ma'am. I just want to enjoy the view a little while longer. No harm in that. There's lousy TV reception out in my cabin and I got nothing else to do."

"Please leave. I warn you, Jess is very protective about his family."

"But you aren't family. What are you? The nanny? I'm guessing that's not all you do around here."

Revulsion crawled up her throat.

She knew the guns were stored under lock and key in Jess's office, the ammunition stored securely somewhere else. Not very handy if Phil made a move.

There was a knife block on the counter behind her, but the risk that he could wrestle one away from her and make it his own weapon was too great to even try.

"Look, I know Jess pays well. Surely you don't

want to throw that away. Just grab your jacket and go. Please."

Phil slowly got out of his chair and strolled toward her like a big cat stalking its prey.

"You're just sooo pretty." He grabbed her arm roughly and hauled her up against his chest. "It isn't fair that he has you all to himself."

She twisted away and backed up, mentally running through the moves she'd learned in her last self-defense class. *Closer. Just a little closer...*

He reached for her again.

With one fluid motion she grabbed his wrist and used his forward momentum to pull him off balance. Rammed her knee into him with every ounce of energy she possessed. When he doubled over, she swiftly twisted his arm behind his back and slammed him to the floor.

"That must hurt," she said with satisfaction. "I wonder if I broke your nose?"

Groaning pitifully, he tried to curl into a fetal position but she shoved his wrist higher along his spine until he yelped and fell limp in defeat.

"I have no words to describe how disgusted I am—or how much I'd like to see a deputy walk through that door right now," she bit out, fishing her cell phone out of her pocket. "But I'm sure I can keep you right here until one does. In fact, I believe I could dislocate your shoulder with just a little more pressure, and I hear that's *really* painful. So don't try anything stupid."

"It won't take long for a deputy to arrive, dear. I called 911 the minute I took the girls to their bedroom. Fortunately, one was patrolling in town." Betty stood in the doorway, her cane in one hand and a rifle in the other, the barrel pointed to the floor.

"Betty!" Abby stared at the rifle, shocked.

"It's loaded," she said primly. "I only ever used it on rattlesnakes too close to the house when my boys were young. I was actually a pretty good shot until I started getting cataracts. Now, I'm afraid I might aim for some nonessential part and accidently hit someone—like Phil, here—in a more serious place. I called Jess, too, by the way. He should be here anytime now."

Five minutes later the back door swung open and Jess strode into the kitchen. His jaw dropped as he swiftly took in Betty's rifle and the scene on the floor. "What's going on?"

Abby rose to her feet slowly, relieved to move away from Phil. Even if she'd thought she had him under control, he still far stronger and heavier than her, and he'd already shown himself to be unpredictable.

He moaned and hauled himself up enough to lean against the cupboards, his eyes closed.

"I never had a good feeling about your ranch

hand, Jess." Betty glared down at Phil. "But tonight I saw him leering at Abby and the girls at supper. Leering—like he was planning something vile while you weren't here to stop him."

"Not true," Phil muttered. "She's lying."

"I put the girls to bed and called you and the sheriff. But then I heard a scuffle. He *attacked* Abby. But by the time I got my rifle unlocked, she already had him on the floor."

Jess pulled Abby into his arms and tucked her head beneath his chin. She melted against the warmth of his chest and the strong beat of his heart. "I am so sorry, Abby. I had no idea Phil was capable of this."

"I'm sorry, too." She pulled back and looked up at him. "In a way, this was my fault."

He frowned. "Your fault?"

"I should have spoken up after his first day, but I didn't think you'd believe me. And I figured I could just handle it. I knew you needed a ranch hand badly."

He gave her a horrified look. "He assaulted you *before* this?"

"No. Until tonight it was only subtle innuendo and crowding my space. Sly compliments that were just a little off." She shuddered. "But tonight, he gave the girls a suggestive look that will haunt me for a long time, then he grabbed me." She rubbed the tender place on her upper arm where he'd gripped her. "Nothing more than a few bruises. I should have told you earlier."

"He would have been fired in an instant, I can promise you that." He dropped a lingering kiss on her lips, sending a shower of sparks through her veins. When the kiss ended, the depth of emotion in his eyes nearly took her breath away.

"I can always look for another hired hand," he added, his voice low and rough. "But the people you love can never be replaced."

Chapter Eighteen

Red and blue lights swirled through the kitchen windows when the deputy finally arrived, followed in a few minutes by another patrol car.

He banged on the back door, and when Jess opened it, the burly deputy was standing to one side with his gun drawn.

"Everything is under control, Bill. Come on in." Jess tipped his head toward Phil, who was still on the floor. "I got tired of keeping an eye on him so I tied him up for you. Early Christmas present."

Soon three more deputies had crowded into the kitchen. Bill shrugged a shoulder. "All of us showing up probably looks like overkill. But domestic situations are dangerous and we don't like to take chances. So, what's going on here?"

By the time Abby finished explaining, Betty had brewed a pot of fresh coffee and plied them all with cookies.

Bill finished writing on his clipboard, then looked between Jess and Abby. "So what we have here is simple assault and an attempted sexual assault. Do you want to press charges?"

"I want him off my property and as far away from here as possible," Jess ground out. "Just thinking about what he wanted to do makes me—"

Abby put her hand on his arm. "I don't know if Phil is a sexual predator, but his background check was clear and that gave him a chance to find potential victims on this ranch." She lifted her chin. "So yes, I want to press charges. I don't want this to happen to anyone else."

Long after the deputies hauled Phil outside and Betty went to bed, Jess sat on the sofa with his arm around Abby's shoulders. The flames flickering in the fireplace sent amber light and dark shadows dancing through the room, adding to the intimacy of the moment.

"When I saw you on the floor, holding that man down, my heart nearly stopped," he murmured. "I'm still amazed at how you handled the situation."

"Yet I doubt anything much will happen to Phil, even though he was arrested. Maybe an overnight at the jail, bail and a suspended sentence at most, and then he'll be on his way." Abby sighed. "But

I couldn't just let it go. I needed to show him that women aren't pushovers."

"He won't be thinking that anytime soon. He got taken down by my grandma and a nanny who barely weighs a hundred pounds." Jess gave her shoulders a little squeeze. "That humiliation has to bite."

"What are you going to do now? With him gone, you're back to working this ranch on your own. Have there been any other applicants?"

"No, but I've handled it all on my own for a long time. With you covering the house and the twins, it won't be hard. If I can find a ranch hand by calving and foaling season, things will be fine."

They both fell silent, watching the fire. After a while Abby's breathing turned slow and even, and he was left to mull over his thoughts...and what he'd said before the patrol cars arrived. *I can always look for another hired hand, but the people you love can never be replaced.*

In that first split second when he'd walked into the house, he'd only registered two things—Abby was in trouble somehow, and she could already be hurt.

Nothing else had mattered. Not the ranch. Not anything he had strived for all his life.

Just her.

His words had come straight from his heart. A truth he'd been denying since the day she'd walked out of his life when they were both just twenty-one.

He brushed a kiss against her golden hair and she stirred, then settled more deeply against his side as the futility of ever spending their future together struck him.

She had dreams. Big dreams. Far beyond what she could ever accomplish on this isolated Montana ranch. A PhD, then research efforts to help those with autism, where her bright mind and determination might make a real difference.

What right did he have to selfishly keep her away from that bright future? She might be tempted to make the wrong choice and the world would not be a better place for it.

He would be grateful for every single day she was here at the ranch. But in the end, he had to make sure she didn't stay.

Abby finished mixing up the herb butter and began working it under the skin of the turkey. She glanced at the recipe she'd printed off the internet. "This really does sound like it'll be nice and moist, doesn't it?"

Betty gave the turkey a jaded glance and continued chopping onions, celery and parsley for the dressing. "Spatchcock, cooking bags, deep fryers—all frippery, in my book. I still like what my mother always did. Just a big ole bird, grease that skin up real good and throw it in the oven. Nothing wrong with that."

Abby hid a smile. "No, of course not."

Jess had taken the girls out to the barn to ride Lollipops and had taken the puppy with them, so the house was surprisingly quiet. Once the turkey was prepared, Abby put it into the oven and wiped down the counters with sanitizer. "It's been a while since I've heard the girls mention their mom."

"It's sad to think of them giving up hope that she'll come back. Yet if Lindsey shows up and whisks them off to California before Christmas, it will really be hard on everyone—even them." Betty dropped a couple sticks of butter into a large pan, waited until they melted, then added the onions, parsley and celery. Soon a wonderful aroma filled the kitchen.

Abby consulted the menu list she'd typed up. "Looks like we're doing really well with everything here. If you're tired, I can take over the dressing so you can put your feet up awhile. We're not eating until three."

Suddenly the house phone rang and Abby's heart skipped a beat. She exchanged glances with Betty. They'd just been talking about Lindsey. What if this was her?

It took several rings before Abby could spur

herself to answer. "The Langfords' Broken Aspen Ranch. This is Abby."

"It's Bill, from the sheriff's department. I'm sorry to have to call you on Thanksgiving, of all days. But I thought you'd want to know. We had your ranch hand in a holding cell, waiting for transfer up to Billings last night. But…well, he overpowered the deputy, knocked him out and got his key ring while being taken out to the squad car."

"So he got out of his handcuffs."

"Yep. We think he's the one who stole a silver SUV from behind the grocery store. The night stocker says he always left his keys in the ignition."

"Are you *looking* for him?"

"We've got an APB out on him and the car. Of course, by now he might have switched vehicles or hopped a bus. But now he's wanted on even more charges, so we'll get him sooner or later."

Abby glanced out the windows at the light snow that had been falling since last night. The landscape was pristine white again, so peaceful. But the thought that Phil might be out there somewhere made her shiver. "You'll call if you hear anything, right?"

"Yes, ma'am. Say *hey* to Jess and his grandma, okay? And if you can pack up Phil's things and put them in the front of his pickup, we'll send someone out to get it. Better to have it in our parking lot than give him a reason to ever come out your way again."

"Thanks." Feeling numb, Abby put down the receiver and turned to Betty. "It was Bill. Phil escaped from jail, and they haven't found him. That's a cheerful thought."

Betty took the saucepan of the buttery, fragrant onion mixture off the stove and poured it over a pile of cubed bread in a roaster pan, then began to lightly stir it together. "Those boys should have been a lot more careful. But now Phil knows what kind of man Jess is, and he won't want to mess with him. And everyone knows ranchers have varmint weapons—if only to protect calves and foals in the spring."

Abby managed a weak smile. "And their grandmas are armed, too. But still."

She thought about the massive, curtainless windows in the living room at night. The way someone could find cover between the highway and the house because of all the pine trees.

If Phil was smart, he would have headed like a rocket out of Montana. *If* he was smart. But she had her doubts.

"I'm going out to the barn to give Jess a heads-up, Betty." She shrugged into her jacket and pulled on her boots. "I'll be back in a couple minutes."

Snow had already blanketed the trees when she

stepped outside, turning the world into a fairyland. To the west, the snow-covered pine forest of the foothills looked like a glittery Christmas card. It would be so hard to leave all of this beauty behind.

In the distance she heard the sound of an approaching diesel motor. *Phil?*

She broke into a jog for the barn. But just as she opened the tack-room door, she looked over her shoulder and recognized the truck as it pulled up next to the barn.

Dad?

He climbed from behind the wheel and met her halfway. "I hope it's okay that we decided to come." He hitched his chin toward Darla, who had stayed in the front seat. "It took some convincing, but this will be good for her. She even made a pie."

Abby enveloped him in a big hug and he awkwardly patted her back in return. "We'll all enjoy having you here. Would you two like to come to the barn with me and see the horses? I just need to tell Jess something."

Dad pursed his lips. "Darla isn't much interested in livestock. Maybe I should just take her on up to the house, if that's all right."

Abby gave Darla a cheerful wave. "Of course it is, Dad. I'll catch up with you two in just a minute."

She watched him get back into his truck and park closer to the house. He opened Darla's door, then took a pie from her and they walked up to the house hand in hand.

Despite Darla's rough edges and prickly attitude, Dad was so sweet, so attentive, that Abby just had to smile.

Would she ever find someone who loved her that much?

She stepped in the warmth and bright light of the tack room and found the twins playing with their puppy. He was now wearing a dress, with a bow taped over one ear. "Where's Uncle Jess?"

Sophie pointed to the door leading to the barn aisle. "He got a phone call. He told us to wait here."

Abby hesitated, then went to the door and stepped into the aisle.

His cell phone propped between his ear and shoulder, Jess was saddling Bart. He looked up at Abby and motioned her to come closer, then ended the call.

"I've got to go. A guy from town was driving past and noticed a silver SUV parked out along the highway. He slowed to see what was going on and the vehicle took off like a shot."

Her stomach knotted. "Phil?"

"My guess is that he wanted revenge before he disappeared, so he opened a pasture gate to cause trouble." Jess checked the cinch one last time. "Now there's a dozen head of cattle wandering along the highway. Drivers coming over the hill might not see them in time to stop, so I've got to get them before someone dies."

"If I hadn't pressed charges, he would've just left town. This is my fault."

Jess turned and put his hands on her shoulders. "Never think that. Phil got what he deserved. Period."

He pulled her close for a moment, brushed a quick kiss on her mouth, then turned away to bridle Bart.

"I'll take the girls up to the house, and then I'll catch up with you. I want to help."

Jess shook his head. "You've got a big dinner going, and Betty will try to do too much. I can handle this."

"It won't be easy by yourself. What if the cattle spook and scatter?"

"Once I get them headed down the ranch lane, they'll have fence on both sides and nowhere else to go but back down here to the barns."

Abby ran for the door. "Dad and Darla just pulled in, so they can take care of things at the house." She called over her shoulder. "I'll be a few minutes behind you."

It took more than a few minutes to take the girls and the puppy to the house and explain the situation. When Abby got back to the barn Jess was gone. But he'd taken a different horse and left

Bart—her favorite—saddled and ready for her. A quiet, thoughtful gesture.

She swung into the saddle and sent Bart into a jog along the shoulder of the lane toward the highway. In the distance she could hear the rumble of a semi engine idling and see its headlights and flashers glowing faintly through the veil of snow.

Amid distant whoops and hollers—voices she didn't recognize—she saw the cattle start coming toward her single file.

She sidestepped Bart farther off the road and watched them pass. Ten. Eleven. Twelve. And then a straggler. Thirteen.

From somewhere behind them she heard Jess call out his thanks to unseen strangers, and then he seemed to materialize through the snowfall like a vision from an old Western movie. A rugged, laconic cowboy on his horse. Competent. Relaxed. Powerful. In command.

She felt transfixed as he drew closer, and it dawned on her that if she never again saw him after she left the ranch, she would never forget this moment. Never forget the way her pulse raced whenever she saw him. And she knew he would always, always possess her heart.

Chapter Nineteen

Abby opened the back door and stepped into the mudroom to shed her boots and coat and closed her eyes in sheer bliss at the aroma of roasted turkey and buttery sage dressing filling the air.

The turkey was already resting on the counter, waiting to be carved, and it smelled like the homemade rolls and dressing were still in the oven but nearly done.

But what captivated her most was the sound of laughter coming from the living room. After washing up, she passed through the dining room—where the table was already set and decorated with candles and a fall flower arrangement that Dad must've brought—and found everyone inside.

Betty and Darla were on the floor in front of the fireplace with the twins, and all four were playing the girls' second-favorite board game, Chinese checkers.

Dad was in one of the leather club chairs, leaning forward with his elbows on his thighs and a big, affectionate grin on his face as Darla purposely flubbed her next turn and gave Sophie the chance to hop two of her marbles.

The crackle of the fire, the aromas of Thanksgiving and the easy camaraderie between the adults and children created such a happy glimpse of family life that Abby felt a catch in her heart. This was everything she'd longed for as an only child.

Jess came up behind her and curved an arm around her waist, just like he would have years ago. "Looks like we've been missing all the fun."

She gave him a teasing nudge with her elbow. "Actually, Bart and I had a *lot* of fun helping with the cattle. It already feels like Christmas out there with that beautiful snow falling."

"Says the girl who doesn't have to actually *deal* with all the snow." He looked down at her, his eyes twinkling. "But thanks again for coming outside. I really did appreciate the company and the help."

The timer on the stove chimed and Betty awkwardly started to rise, but Darla shook her head. "I'll get that and start putting things on the counter. You've worked too hard already."

Abby followed her. "I'll help. Just tell me what to do."

"Um…can you carve the turkey? I'm not very good at that." Darla scanned the kitchen. "Otherwise, the mashed potatoes are done and staying warm in the slow cooker. Betty already made the turkey gravy. The fruit salad and broccoli salad are in the fridge, and I'm ready to pull the dressing, sweet potato casserole and rolls from the oven."

Abby pulled a carving knife from the knife block and got to work. "I honestly didn't expect to put you to work like this, but I really appreciate all of your help."

"I was happy to do it. Don and I would have been home alone otherwise, and this is so much more fun. I'm afraid he and I aren't very good cooks, but we fumbled through making the mashed potatoes and the sweet-potato casserole. If they didn't turn out, it's all our fault." Darting a quick, tentative glance at Abby, Darla started pulling food from the oven and resting each of the pans on trivets set along the longest counter. "Betty says she always sets up a buffet in here for holidays because it's just easier. Is that okay with you?"

"She's the boss, not me. I'm just the hired help." Abby grinned at her, both surprised and relieved at Darla's demeanor. Until now she'd been brittle and defensive, but now she seemed almost… happy. "A buffet sounds like a good idea."

Darla bustled around the kitchen putting out the food, finding ladles and serving spoons. She stood back and looked at all of the food filling the counter, and at the end, four pies and a plate of cookies. "Wow. I've only seen a Thanksgiving spread like this in magazines. I didn't realize people actually did all of this."

"Do you miss being with your own family today?" Abby asked gently.

Darla cut a glance at her, then looked down. "There's no one left, really. My brother died in Iraq a long time ago. My mom and dad have been gone even longer."

"I'm so sorry."

"I know what you think of me. What everyone in town thinks." Darla's voice caught. "But I promise you, marrying Don was never about his ranch or his money. He's just so kind and thoughtful. I never met anyone like him. And he doesn't have a mean bone in his body. He's the first man in my life who ever treated me like a real lady."

"Then I think he must love you very much."

Darla took a shaky breath. "I love him so much that I would die for him."

Abby thought about the one man she'd ever really loved. The one she would never have. "Believe me, I understand. I—"

The twins burst into the kitchen. "Is it time? Can we eat now? Everything smells so good!"

"Thanks to Betty and Darla, I think we're all ready." Abby reached for Darla's hand and squeezed it gently, thankful for the interruption before she'd said too much. "Let's all hold hands and say grace."

She waited a moment, then began. "Thank You, Lord, for this wonderful family gathering. For Darla and Dad, who have joined us today. We hope this will be the start of many more dinners together. Thank You for Betty and Darla, who have made such a beautiful meal, and for Your healing and grace that has brought Betty back to this ranch. We give thanks for the two little girls with us, and ask that You shower them with blessings now and forever. And we thank You for Jess, who works so hard and provides such a wonderful example of what a father should be. Finally, please bless this food, our companionship today and the coming weeks of preparation for Jesus's birth. Amen."

A chorus of *amens* joined hers, and then she stepped back. "Let's let Bella and Sophie go first. I'll help them with their plates. Then just grab a plate from the table, everyone, and come on through."

Betty joined Darla and Abby at the stove as the men went through after the twins.

"I want to thank you both again," Darla said quietly, looking down at her hands. "It meant a lot to Don and I to be here today. It's been…quiet, for us, since we got married."

Abby looked over at Betty and raised an eyebrow.

It wasn't hard to read between the lines. There'd been no well-wishers calling on the newlyweds. No dinner invitations or cheerful chats outside church. And Darla, who'd never lived here before, must still feel isolated and alone.

Betty turned to Darla. "I realize now that I've been a terrible neighbor to someone so new to Pine Bend. All of us have."

Darla gave her a startled look. "I—I don't know what you mean."

"I'd like to introduce you to some people you might enjoy. We'll start by picking you and Don up for church next Sunday. And, maybe you could help me and some of the other ladies with the refreshments for the Sunday School Christmas program. Then you'll meet more of the younger ladies."

Abby smiled to herself as she headed to the dining room to check on the twins.

Under Betty's wing, it would be no time at all until Darla became a part of the community—and perhaps even busier than she wanted to be.

"I am *still* thinking about that wonderful Thanksgiving meal," Jess said, looking over Lucy's withers at Abby. "I think it was the best ever."

Her cheeks rosy from the cold, she looked down at him from atop Bart and laughed. "I'm sure it isn't too hard remembering it, since we're still eating the leftovers."

"And I'm glad." Jess lifted Sophie up and settled her in front of Abby, then mounted Lucy and leaned down to pick up Bella. "Are you ready?"

"We're really going to cut down a Christmas tree? A *real* one?" Sophie wiggled with excitement. "We never done that before."

"And you girls get to pick which one," he reassured her. "Unless you can't agree. Then Abby and I will need to help."

They rode side by side up into the north pasture where he knew there would be plenty of blue spruce to choose from.

"You've been planting them, I see," Abby said as she surveyed the field up ahead.

"Dad started years ago. He would plant a dozen or so every year and I've kept up the tradition. Of course not all survive and some have grown way too big, but they're beautiful all the same, and we always have good trees to choose from."

Bella pointed excitedly to a tree off to the right that had to be eighteen feet tall. "That one, Uncle Jess. That one there!"

"It is beautiful. But it's too tall and wide. It wouldn't fit. We need to find something nine feet or under, with a straight trunk so it will stand up nicely in the house. How about you, Sophie? Do you see anything?"

She shook her head.

"Abby?"

"Don't ask me. I think this should be the girls' decision."

They rode up and down the hills, past dozens of trees of every shape and size. Everything the girls liked was too tall, too wide to get through the door or too gnarled to stand up straight, until Bella suddenly pointed to one farther up the hill.

"That one!" She screamed with delight. "It's so pretty!"

Jess studied it long and hard. "You know what, I think you might be right. That is a fine tree. What do you think, Sophie?"

Sophie's lower lip trembled. "Not that one."

Abby gave her a hug. "So what do you like? Do you see something pretty?"

She nodded, and pointed to a small, scraggly tree they'd passed earlier. "That one."

Jess and Abby reined the horses toward the tree and stopped next to it.

"That is a sweet little tree," Abby ventured. "But maybe it needs more time to grow. What do you all think?"

"That's not a pretty tree *at all*," Bella announced stubbornly. "I don't want that one."

"But I do," Sophie said sadly. "No one else will

ever love it 'cause it's not pretty enough and it will always be lonely."

Abby and Jess exchanged glances, and Jess felt a little catch in his throat. This wasn't about a small, wind-battered tree. It was about a little girl's heart, and maybe a fear that she'd been left because she wasn't good enough.

"You know what? I think it would be perfect to bring both trees back. What do you say? The big one could go in the living room, and the girls could decide where they'd like the smaller one."

"Yes, please," Sophie whispered. "It needs a home."

Jess dismounted and handed his reins to Abby, then pulled a folding camping saw from one of his saddlebags and untied his lariat from the front of his saddle. In no time, he had both trees cut down and trussed so he could drag them behind his horse.

Abby reached into one of the saddlebags behind her own saddle and pulled out a thermos, plus some small paper coffee cups with plastic lids. "Who wants some hot cocoa?"

She handed them out to Bella and Sophie, then filled a larger cup for Jess. "I always wanted to do this when I was a little girl—ride up into the foothills on horseback and bring back a Christmas tree. My dad always went out with his tractor and brought one back, and my mom had it decorated when I woke up the next morning."

Sophie turned to look up at her. "Can we decorate our trees? I'd like that. Bella would, too."

Abby gave her a hug. "Of course, sweetie. I think that would be a lot more fun. I'm not sure if we can get it done tonight, though. When we get home, you need to go to town for your first Christmas-program practice at the church, and after that will be supper. Jess?"

"We'll see. Maybe we can put up both trees today and at least decorate the smaller one." His phone chimed. He looked at the screen and turned away to take the call.

After a few minutes, he got back on his horse, avoiding Abby's curious expression.

This wasn't anything to discuss in front of the girls. He wasn't even sure he wanted to tell Abby, because she'd probably blame herself. And sad as this was, it definitely wasn't her fault.

After they got back to the ranch, Jess brought the big tree into the house and got it set up in its tree stand, then let the girls help him bring the smaller tree into their room, the puppy romping beside them as if he thought they'd just brought him the world's biggest toy.

"So, what do you think?" he asked.

The girls nodded. They'd both wanted it in the

far corner, so they could sit up in bed and see it when hearing their nightly stories.

Bella gave him a heartfelt look. "Can we put on the lights? Please?"

"We need to leave in just fifteen minutes," Abby said, looking at her watch. "I made chili in the slow cooker, so everything will be ready after we get home from church. We can have an early supper, and then there'll be plenty of time to decorate your tree before bed."

"I'll take the girls to town." Jess adjusted the tree and picked up a few stray pine needles from the floor. "But I need to talk to you for minute first."

The phone call.

Had it been the girls' mother saying she was on her way? Someone who he'd hired to become the new nanny? Whoever it was, she'd seen the expression on Jess's face and knew this couldn't be good.

Abby hesitated in the doorway. "Girls, you need to wash your hands and faces and change your clothes before we go back to church. As soon as you're ready we need to leave."

With the puppy at her heels, she sought out Jess in the living room, where Betty was napping under an afghan in her favorite chair, then looked in the kitchen, and finally found him at his desk.

He looked up, his expression grave. "Where are the girls?"

"Washing up and changing their clothes. I figured you would want them occupied for this. What's up?"

"Phil did steal that silver SUV in town the night he escaped. And…it apparently was him parked out on the highway on Thanksgiving when the gate was opened."

"None of this is a surprise. We figured as much."

He nodded. "Well…when we got that call from a passerby about the loose cattle he must've realized he'd been spotted, because he took off. He passed a patrol car in the next county doing ninety, so the deputy went after him. Then Phil went around a corner and disappeared."

Abby felt a queasy sensation in her stomach. "So he could still be in the area?"

"The snow was falling heavily enough to hide his tracks on the side of the road. Some cross-country skiers called 911 this morning to report a car in a ravine, the driver deceased. Phil must have skidded, hit a guardrail and gone airborne."

Abby dropped into a chair in front of the desk. "I…don't know what to say. If I hadn't—"

"None of us would have wished him harm. But he chose his actions. He escaped. He chose to come back here for a little revenge, and he chose to run from the law."

"Do…do you have anything on his job application about his family? Someone to contact?" Abby closed her eyes briefly, imagining the family that would mourn him.

"That's where it gets interesting. A deputy told me that Phil's name didn't match his fingerprints. Apparently he had quite a rap sheet and was wanted for theft, so he was using a stolen identity. That's why he tried so hard to escape."

"But what about his references?"

"Faked. The phone number I called probably belonged to a buddy who vouched for him."

"I'm just sorry this happened."

"You did the right thing, Abby, and I'm grateful. The thought of him so much as *looking* at you and the girls makes me angry. And I'm even more angry at myself for not realizing what kind of man he was."

Jess had always been a protector—the kind of man who cared about family more than himself and did what was right. That he'd immediately believed her words about Phil and now shouldered the blame for the man's presence was just one more facet of Jess that she would never forget.

The woman who won him over would be the most fortunate woman on earth. Abby just wished it could be her.

Chapter Twenty

The house phone rang minutes after Jess left with the girls for the Christmas-program rehearsal. After checking the caller ID, Abby picked up the receiver. "Darla! It's so nice to hear from you."

"Don thought we should come over to tell you, but I thought maybe calling was better. Are you busy? I can call tomorrow or later this week."

From the tentative tone in her voice, Abby guessed this call hadn't been easy to make. "Now is good. What's up?"

A long pause.

"We had a wonderful time on Thanksgiving. Thanks so much for the invitation. I've never had such a great meal. And...um...it was so nice of y'all to pick up Don and me for church this morning. It was much easier than walking in alone, and..."

In the background, Abby heard a gentle warning in Dad's voice. "Darla, go ahead. Tell her."

"Um, anyway—Don got a phone call an hour ago, but he was out doing chores, and the caller said I could help him just fine."

Even over the phone, Abby could hear Darla swallow hard.

"He said he was your ex and that he was calling Don because he needed to find you. I wouldn't have told him anything except he seemed to know both of you really well, so I figured he was telling the truth about who he was."

"*Alan* called?"

"Yeah. I told him you were at the Langford ranch. Then he said you were going to be really happy because things were gonna change. And that he looked forward to seeing you real soon, and then he asked for the Langford phone number and I gave it to him. I just didn't think. Afterward I realized that surely he would have your cell number, right? And if you wanted him to have the ranch number, you would've already given it to him. I am so sorry."

This news hit Abby with the force of a straight-line wind—too fast to really catch. Abby blinked. "You're right. Alan should have my cell number. This doesn't make sense."

"When I told Don, he said Alan was the last guy you'd ever want to hear from."

The poor woman sounded so rattled that Abby wished they *had* come in person, so she could give Darla a reassuring hug.

"Don said…" There was a long pause, and Abby heard her father's voice in the background again. "He doesn't want me to repeat it. But I don't think he likes Alan very much."

"Believe me, I know that's an understatement," Abby said dryly. The puppy pawed at her leg and she bent down to pick him up and snuggle her cheek against his soft, fluffy fur. "But for what it's worth, tell Dad that he was right about Alan all along."

"We just wanted you to know in case Alan does call. Or turns up at the ranch or something."

"That's all right. No worries," Abby said quietly. "I'm not upset, just confused. He's the one who filed for divorce. What little we had together was divided up largely in his favor. And the last time I saw him, he was boasting about moving in with the woman he fell love with. Why would he call me now?"

"I don't know. I just hope you aren't mad at me," Darla said softly.

"Of course I'm not. And now we're related, so don't give this a second thought. Don't forget—we all hope you'll join us for Christmas."

"We'd love that. Lanna will be at her dad's, and it would be so quiet with just the two of us."

Abby chuckled. "Hopefully we won't have another cattle roundup in the middle of the food preparations, but you never know."

After setting the table for dinner, Abby poured a mug of coffee, put some cookies on a plate and took it out to the living room for Betty. "Need a little something to tide you over until supper?"

"Oh, my. That looks so good." Betty set aside a lapful of pink knitting yarn. "Can you join me for a bit?"

Abby went back to the kitchen for a cup of coffee and settled onto one of the sofas with a sigh of pleasure.

Betty nodded approvingly. "You should sit down more often. You don't need to be bustling around all the time. The house will always wait."

"And get worse and worse…"

"But with two little girls it's never going to be tidy all the time. Just wait till Jess gets out all of our boxes of Christmas decorations. Twelve of them, I think."

"What little I have is in storage back in Chicago. I didn't ever have much, though. Alan wasn't really into the holidays."

Betty pursed her lips. "Speaking of him, I couldn't help but overhear that phone call. Didn't mean to, of course, but I have ears like a bat when my hearing aids are in. Sounds like he's quite a doozy."

"He had his good points," Abby said carefully.

"I sure hope he was good-looking, because it sounds like he's lacking on the things that count."

Abby tried and failed to suppress a laugh. "You do know how to cut to the chase."

Betty shook a forefinger at her. "You aren't thinking of going back to him, I hope. You're a much smarter girl than that."

"Smart enough to never even consider it, I promise." Abby thought about Jess and Maura, who were at the church right now. Wrangling small children on stage for the nativity play, or trying to teach them to sing "Away in a Manger." Perhaps Maura was even trying to patch up their old relationship in the process.

"That one mistake of yours doesn't mean there can't be a perfectly good match elsewhere." Betty gave Abby a stern look. "Here, for instance."

"I'm finding that being single is far better than a bad marriage. And since I wasn't a good judge the last time around, I think I'll enjoy unwedded bliss for the rest of my days."

"Hmm. You just haven't been married to the right man yet. Now Jess, for instance—"

"I think he'll be well occupied when I leave, Betty."

Betty pulled a face. "And who in the world would that be?"

Abby gave a little shrug. How Betty could have

missed Maura's determined efforts at church was hard to fathom. "Now that you're done with your PT appointments, how are you feeling? You seem to get around well with your cane."

"Changing subjects won't change the facts, young lady." Betty harrumphed again, and pulled her knitting back into her lap. "You and Jess belong together, yet you're determined to waste a wonderful opportunity. Mark my words, you'll have only yourselves to blame."

After supper Jess hauled two more boxes of decorations from the attic. When Abby brought the last box down, they could all get to work decorating.

This would be the girls' first Christmas here. Maybe their last. And Abby would be gone well before next Christmas.

He forced himself to think about *this* Christmas. The one he would remember forever.

He'd already resolved to do everything in his power to make it special, though he wasn't sure what that entailed exactly, beyond what he'd seen on TV. A fairyland of Christmas lights in the yard covering every tree and every angle of the house? An explosion of presents under the tree?

The last truly joyous Christmas Jess remembered at the ranch had been the year before four-year-old Heather died. She'd been killed just months before Christmas, and that year there had been only tears and sorrow. Less than a year later Mom died. After that, Dad had never again looked at the holidays as a time for joy, and Grandma Betty had tried to pick up the pieces as best she could, bless her heart.

The sound of Betty thumping across the floor with her cane brought Jess out of his thoughts. She tapped one of the boxes. "Christmas tree lights in that one," she announced. "And the one next to it is filled with ornaments. If you can bring those two down to the twins' room, we'll get started."

Abby appeared with the last storage box. "This one says Christmas Linens. Should I put it in the dining room?"

Betty nodded again. "That one has the big Christmas-angel tree topper in it, so be careful."

Down in the girls' bedroom, Bella and Sophie were playing with the puppy as they waited impatiently. Abby turned on Christmas music on her iPod, then joined Betty and the girls to watch Jess wind the light strands around and around the tree.

When he plugged them in, the tree lit up with bright multicolored lights.

"Okay girls, here are some ornaments," Jess said as he pried open the other storage box. "Use whatever you want."

"*All* of them?" Sophie asked with a shy smile.

Jess nodded. He stepped back and let the girls

do it all except for the very highest branches. His heart expanded as he watched them, their faces shining in the warm light of the tree and their eyes sparkling with joy. The innocence of childhood. The trust that dreams would always come true.

Bella tugged on his sleeve. "Are you sad, Uncle Jess? Christmas is 'sposed to be happy."

He swung her up in his arms. "Of course it is, punkin. I was just thinking about how much I want this to be a very, very merry Christmas for everyone."

"Abby says we're making Christmas cookies after school tomorrow."

He tapped her nose lightly with his forefinger. "Well, that makes *me* happy, because you girls are the very best cookie bakers in the whole world."

She beamed at him proudly, then flung her slender arms around his neck. "I love you, Uncle Jess. With my whole heart."

"I love you, too, sweetie, *both* of you," he murmured. He scooped Sophie up into his arms, too. "You'll never know how much."

Her eyes rounded. "Hundreds and thousands?"

He couldn't help but smile. To Bella, that meant any number beyond how high she could count. "Hundred and thousands," he repeated solemnly. "And forever and ever."

Chapter Twenty-One

With Christmas Eve less than two weeks away, every day seemed to be filled with wonder. What had his life been like before two little girls appeared and turned it upside down?

Jess didn't want to remember.

Now they were bringing home art projects from school that Abby taped all over the kitchen: lacy cutout snowflakes. Construction-paper reindeer with red noses. Chalky drawings of snowy winter scenes. Tipsy-looking cotton-ball snowmen.

And the baking continued every day, filling the house with tempting aromas. Sometimes Darla came over and helped Betty, Abby and the girls make Christmas cookies he'd never seen before, each more colorful and delicious than the last. All meant to give the girls more memories of a warm and happy kitchen where they were loved and treasured.

It had been six weeks since Lindsey's call and her promise to come by Christmas, and it felt as if a clock was ticking away the hours and days way too fast.

Jess had left church early that morning—right after the sermon and offering—to meet an out-of-state horse-training client traveling through Montana who wanted to see the progress Jess was making with a three-year-old mare.

After the man left, Jess went back to the chores he'd started at dawn. If only he could find a good, decent ranch hand.

A few minutes later his cell phone chimed.

The screen showed an unfamiliar number from out of state. *Probably not my perfect ranch hand*, he sighed as he answered the call. "Broken Aspen Ranch, Jess Langford speaking."

"Good. This is Alan Halliday."

Jess had never met the guy, but the cloying, smug tone in the man's voice and his arrogant manner set Jess's teeth on edge. "Can I help you?"

"I understand Abby is at your ranch. Just like old times?" The innuendo in his voice came through loud and clear.

Did he imagine Abby had come to Montana to pick right back up where things had ended twelve years ago? "She's *working* here, yes."

Alan laughed. "She's quite a gal, as long as you watch your back. You know, she dumped me when my health got rough. Pretty shallow, really. But maybe you'll have better luck."

Jess bit back a sharp response and counted to ten. "I'm not sure why you've called. But—"

"She had second thoughts after she left, and begged me to take her back. But of course I wouldn't," Alan said. "At least not then. Just tell her something for me."

"And that is…?"

"I've learned that our divorce wasn't actually finalized after all…thanks to my stupid lawyer, who didn't properly file the papers. But tell her that I've been thinking that maybe this was a message from above, and I've been considering giving her another chance. Tell her to call me."

He rattled off a phone number and hung up.

Aghast that this man would share so much personal information with a stranger, Jess stood staring down the barn aisle, his hands shaking. If Alan had been telling him these things about Abby in person, it would've been hard to keep from throttling him.

Jess had known Abby throughout grade school, high school and college. He'd loved her then and he loved her still. How could Alan be so totally wrong?

And how on earth had Abby stayed with someone like him for so long?

At the sound of a familiar vehicle pulling to a

stop, Jess went outside. "Abby—can I talk to you a minute?"

Betty and the girls waved to him and went on to the house. Abby waited, her long blond hair waving down the back of her red jacket like a waterfall. "What's up? Is anything wrong?"

"You had a phone call from Alan. He wants you to call him." He held out a piece of paper. "Here's the number, if you need it."

She eyed it like it might be a rattler ready to strike. "Thanks, but no."

"He claims his lawyer botched something with your divorce paperwork, and says it isn't final."

She looked at him with horror. "What? But that's not possible." She bit her lower lip. "At least I don't think so."

"I don't know him," Jess said, carefully choosing his words. "But after talking to him for a few minutes, I think you might want to check with your lawyer first."

"If there's really a problem with the divorce, my lawyer can handle it. She can also remind Alan's lawyer that I want no further contact. Period."

Jess hesitated, debating about how much to say. "Well, just so you're prepared, I don't think he was joking when he told me that the paperwork problem might be a sign. He said that he *might* give you another chance."

She stared at Jess for a moment, then laughed.

"Over my dead body. Honestly, what is he thinking? He's the one who demanded the divorce, not me."

"One other thing. He seemed happy that I was the one who answered the landline phone, and then he proceeded to share some negative things about you."

"Something must have happened between him and his new girlfriend. And now he's trying to make sure that he gets his breadwinner back. Me." She turned her gaze to the sky, as if looking for answers. "It will never happen. Have you ever wondered how you could have been so incredibly blind about someone?"

"Yes, I have." He'd been blind to the treasure in his life, the girl he'd lost, who was now standing before him. "I want you to know that I don't believe a word of what Alan said. He doesn't deserve someone like you."

She rested a hand against his cheek. "Thank you, Jess," she whispered softly. "I'd honestly forgotten what it's like to have someone believe in me."

Every day after school, the twins helped decorate the house until every surface seemed to be adorned with wreaths, Christmas figurines, snow globes and Betty's collection of nativity sets. Christmas stockings hung by the fire.

Jess continued to string lights outside until the house and the entire yard twinkled. Pine boughs wrapped with Christmas lights covered the railings of the wraparound porch, and Jess had even hung a giant wreath above the wide sliding door of the horse barn that Abby could see from the living-room windows.

Abby cleared the lunch dishes from the table, then went to find Betty and the girls.

Betty looked up from the card table she'd placed in front of her chair by the fire. "One left. For now."

Abby laughed. "Another one?"

"Tradition," she said firmly. "One can't have enough."

Betty had been busy this week creating pretty little clusters of mistletoe to hang above the top step leading into the covered porch and in every doorway. There was mistletoe everywhere, and her intentions were clear, even if she continued to deny them with an innocent smile.

Abby felt a rush of cold air come billowing in from the kitchen as Jess came in the back door. "I've got my SUV warming up. Who's ready to go to town?"

The twins came running for their coats and boots.

Betty shook her head. "I think I'll stay nice and warm right here."

"But, Gramma," Sophie cried, coming back to tug on Betty's hand. "You hafta come. Santa is there. And Uncle Jess says everything will be pretty."

"I'll be at your Christmas program at church tomorrow, I promise. I'm just not sure I'm ready to face the slippery sidewalks in town just yet."

"You're sure?" Abby brushed a kiss against Betty's parchment cheek. "I can hold on to you."

"I have a feeling those girls will be mighty excited to see the window decorations and meet Santa, so you go along. You can text me some pictures, if you like."

By the time Jess found a parking spot near Main Street, the sidewalks were filled with shoppers. Wreaths and ribbons festooned all of the lampposts, and every shop window had been decorated. Christmas carolers strolled the street, filling the air with their music.

"This is really beautiful," Abby said with wonder. "I don't remember any of this when I was growing up."

Jess nodded. "The town has a lot more shopping on Main now. The Saturday before Christmas is the biggest celebration of the year."

They followed the girls as they ran from one shop window to the next. Most of them displayed pretty winter and Christmas scenes, with figures that moved and trains that chugged on their tracks through the display. In some of the doorways, clerks dressed as holiday characters passed out candy canes.

Snow started falling, and the twins stopped to tip their heads back to try to catch the flakes on their tongue.

"I wonder if they'll remember the snow?"

Abby looked up and caught a hint of sadness in Jess's eyes. She threaded her arm through the crook of his elbow and lowered her voice. "You don't know for sure that they'll go back to California. Lindsey might not even come. Maybe you can pursue custody. But either way, they'll always remember this, Jess. No matter what happens. They'll look back and remember that this was a wonderful year."

"I hope so." He looked down at her. "I know that I'll never forget."

He looked as if he wanted to say something more, but Bella and Sophie had reached the next corner and were shouting and waving at them. The moment was lost.

Across the street, an empty lot had been turned into a North Pole village, with a red-and-white-striped Santa house adorned with bright green pillars in front and a reindeer pen to one side. Santa sat in a chair in full regalia, with a line of several dozen children waiting to talk to him.

Sophie slipped her mittened hand into Abby's and looked up at her. "Can I tell you a secret?"

Abby crouched down in front of her. "Of course you can."

"My momma said she doesn't believe in Santa. She said nothing ever good happens, even if you ask. 'Cause he isn't real."

Abby glanced up at Jess, then cradled the child's cheek in her hand. "But you still want to go see Santa?"

"And Bella, too. We both have to. But we can't tell you what we ask for."

"Then that's what we should do. Right, Uncle Jess?"

He nodded and took Bella's hand, and they crossed the street to get in line. When it was the girls' turn to see Santa, Abby took out her phone to take pictures and texted them to Betty.

On the way back to the SUV, they stopped at each store window on the other side of the street.

"Do you girls see anything you'd like for Christmas?" Abby asked, pointing at an array of lifelike dolls. "Something like that?"

The girls shook their heads.

"What about that big dollhouse? Or that art set?" No matter what Abby pointed out, they only shook their heads. By the time they reached the SUV, she'd given up. "Well, then, can you tell me what you *would* like for Christmas? It's only a few days away, so you need to decide."

"It's a secret," Bella said. "But Santa knows. And he said our wish would come true."

Chapter Twenty-Two

Jess headed for his office after they got back from town, feeling a moment of trepidation as he looked at his answering machine.

It was blinking.

He held his breath and checked the screen, exhaling his relief at a Montana area code. Another reprieve. Tapping the Play button, he leaned back in his chair.

A calm, mature voice introduced itself as Helen Peabody, and she wanted to apply for the housekeeper-nanny position. She'd already emailed her resume. She sounded responsible. Kindly. Perfect. Exactly like the type of employee he had been searching for when Abby suddenly appeared at the rehab center with her big blue eyes and sweet laughter.

He found Helen's email and the attached resume in his inbox. He was just printing it when he heard a knock at his office door.

Abby came into the room and plopped down in one of the club chairs facing his desk. "I have a pretty good idea about what the girls want for Christmas."

"I'm afraid I do, too." He pulled the résumé from the printer tray and laid it on the corner of his desk. It fluttered to the floor. "Lindsey."

"What are you going to do?"

"After she called to say she was coming I tried to make an appointment with my lawyer, but he's been in Florida most of December dealing with his mother's estate and property dispersal. I'll be meeting with him right after Christmas, as well as someone from Montana Social Services."

"Good decision, Jess. At least then you'll know where you stand." Abby rose, bent down to pick up the stray sheet of paper on the floor and put it back on his desk. "I guess I'd better get back to work."

Her gaze fell on the paper as she turned to go. She did a double take, and then she looked up at him. "Have you found a new ranch hand?"

"They don't generally show up with resumes, unfortunately." He cleared his throat. "This one is from someone applying to be a housekeeper. She actually sounds really good."

"Then you'll need to make sure she doesn't get

away." Abby tipped her head and met his gaze squarely. "That's good news, right?"

He swallowed. "Abby—"

She was already out the door.

As always, the weather was changeable in this part of Montana during December—ranging from gentle snowfalls to bitter blizzards, with balmy interludes in between.

By Sunday morning another storm had barreled in with sixty-mile-an-hour winds and heavy snow, and both church this morning and the evening children's Christmas program were cancelled.

The twins were devastated.

"Maura just called, and she has arranged everything with the pastor," Abby reassured them at bedtime. "You'll have your children's program at the Christmas Eve service instead. I still can't wait to see what you girls are doing."

Bella nodded firmly. "We promised not to tell."

"I know, and you are *very* good at keeping secrets."

After reading a stack of books, Abby and Betty said their prayers with the girls and kissed them good-night.

"Sleep tight, everyone. I'm heading off to bed," Betty said.

"And me, too. Pretty soon, anyway." Abby

scooped the puppy from Bella's bed and went out to sit by the fire with a cup of hot strawberry tea.

The fire and the twinkling lights on the Christmas tree in the corner lit the room with a lovely glow, and the soft instrumental Christmas music in the background filled her with a sense of peace.

In just two nights it would be Christmas Eve.

Dad and Darla were coming over after the church service for a light dinner and the opening of presents, staying overnight; then on Christmas morning everyone would pitch in to make a big Christmas dinner. One big, happy family.

It was what she'd always longed for while growing up as an only child.

Well, she would finally have her big family Christmas, but then she'd soon be on her way. She fingered the folded business letter in her front shirt pocket and took it out. Even after reading it three times, it still gave her a little thrill of excitement…and a dose of melancholy.

At the sound of Jess coming in the back door, she debated slipping off to her room instead of staying to make awkward conversation.

The housekeeper's resume on his desk had reminded her once again of just how temporary her situation was. It had been all too easy to think of Jess and her together, and with every passing day she'd found more to love about the man he'd become.

But now, with a promising new housekeeper coming for an interview, it would soon be time for Abby to slip away, even if it broke her heart.

Jess came into the living room in his stocking feet, his face reddened from the cold wind and his dark hair tousled by the stocking cap he'd worn.

He sank into the sofa nearest the fireplace, propped his elbows on his thighs and shoved his unruly hair back from his forehead.

"You look tired, Jess. Can I get you some hot cocoa? Coffee?"

Abby started to stand, but he waved her back down. "I'm fine. I just want to warm up awhile."

"Is the drive clear?"

He nodded. Leaned back against the sofa and closed his eyes. "For now. If the wind picks up, I'll have to do it all over again tomorrow."

"It's hard to believe Christmas is almost here," she murmured, staring into the fire. "Have you heard from your brothers?"

He rolled his head against the cushion to look at her. "The last time Devlin came home was for Dad's funeral, and he never comes home for Christmas. He's always off at some military base or in the Middle East somewhere, though he did email and say he might come back for a while this spring. Tater—uh, Tate—sent an email saying he'd be spending Christmas with his new girlfriend and her family in Cheyenne. Every year it's a different girlfriend. I think it's just an excuse not to come home."

Abby laughed. "Do you still call him Tater to his face?"

"Not often. Only if I've been missing our old wrestling matches out on the lawn. But now he's as tall as me and in better shape, so it's not as much fun."

"I still see both of your brothers as gangly, awkward teenagers. Time flies, I guess." She folded and refolded the letter in her hands. "Did I tell you that I got some news?"

Jess's dark eyebrows drew together. "Alan?"

"The only news I want from him would be through my lawyer. Yesterday I got a letter from a university out east."

He sat up straighter and turned toward her. "You were accepted?"

She nodded, trying to generate the excitement and enthusiasm he would expect. "The financial-aid package is pretty sweet. They're giving me a research assistantship that will cover tuition and insurance, and a medical corporation has awarded me an additional grant that will help with living expenses. I'll start spring term. But they…uh… suggest that I come out early to find housing and get settled. I couldn't ask for more."

Though it would be impossibly far from the people she loved. Yet, a blessing in itself, really.

How hard would it be to stay in this area and see Jess with someone else, raising the twins and their own children?

"That's wonderful. Really wonderful. I'm happy for you, Abby. Truly." Jess stood up and nodded in her direction, then headed down the hall toward his office and beyond that, his bedroom.

She felt her heart shatter a little more with each step he took.

When she heard his door shut, she turned away to unplug the Christmas tree lights and scatter the remaining embers in the fireplace until they winked out, one by one. Just like her silly hopes and dreams.

What had she expected—a declaration of undying love? A plea that she never leave? That was the stuff of fairy tales, not real life.

And certainly not hers.

Chapter Twenty-Three

Jess looked up from his computer screen when Betty walked into his office the next morning, her face a mask of worry. "What's wrong?"

"Nothing… Not really. It's just… I just can't help worrying about that granddaughter of mine. Here it's already Christmas Eve tomorrow and Lindsey hasn't even called. Either she's the most thoughtless mother ever or something terrible has happened to her."

He rounded the desk and took her arm as she settled into one of the club chairs, then he sat next to her. "I've been worried, too. I tried calling her stepmother this morning but didn't get an answer. And I also checked in again with the Los Angeles Police Department to see if they knew anything. But it's always the same. Nothing."

"I want her to be safe and well. Truly I do." Betty gripped his arm. "But what if she takes those little girls back to California? Can you imagine? I still can't believe they were left alone in that apartment overnight. In a *closet*. Who would do such a terrible thing? And what about the bruises they had? I'd rather run away with them myself than let that happen again."

He rested his hand on top of hers. "I'm going to do my best to make sure it doesn't. I promise you that."

"I've been praying about this every day. But I suppose I started worrying more lately because I thought Lindsey would have shown up by now. And surely by Christmas, don't you think?" She wearily rose to her feet. "I'd better get back to the kitchen and finish my pies. Sorry if I bothered you."

"You are never a bother, Grandma." He gave her a kiss on her cheek. "If you need any help tasting those pies, just give me a shout."

As she hobbled toward the door with her cane, the twins peeked into his office, their eyes wide. Then he heard them thunder down the hallway.

The last two days they'd either been scampering through the house with their puppy or shaking presents under the Christmas tree, all the more excited because Christmas Eve was just around the corner. And probably a little stir-crazy, too, with all of the snow and cold keeping them inside.

Christmas. Because of the twins, he was more excited about it this year than he'd been in all the years since he'd grown up. He just hoped it would be perfect for everyone.

Yet—like Grandma Betty, he'd been worrying. A lot.

He'd prayed more this winter than he had since he was a child. He'd been trying to just give those worries over to God and trust that the right answers would come. That the two innocent little girls would be safe and secure…and that their troubled mother would be, too.

But there seemed to be no perfect answer. And no one would be left unscathed if a custody battle ensued. He just hoped God—with His infinite wisdom—had it all worked out.

Abby finished wrapping a present in her room and carried the small stack out to the Christmas tree to join the others she'd placed there earlier.

She lowered the volume of the Christmas instrumental music and suddenly realized that the entire house was quiet. Too quiet.

She took a quick walk down the hall to Betty's room, but she was snoozing and no little girls seemed to be hiding there. Her own room. The extra guest rooms. The twins' bedroom.

Nothing.

Concerned now, she searched the other rooms on the main floor, then even searched the unfinished basement.

The shadows outside were growing longer—

and it would soon be dark. Gusts of wind lifted and swirled the snow drifts outside, and the temp was already dropping into the minus digits. It would be an evening to stay nice and warm inside. Where were they?

She glanced back at the kitchen and the little coat pegs set at child height. Her heart skipped a beat. Their coats and boots were gone.

"Jess! *Jess!*"

He reached the kitchen before she had a chance to grab her coat.

"The girls—I can't find them anywhere. Their coats are gone. They've never gone outside alone. And it's cold, and it's getting dark—"

He rested his hands on her shoulders. "I'll go outside and start in the horse barn. I want you to check the house one more time and then come out. Okay?"

She nodded, fighting back her tears. "Why would they take off like this?"

"Don't worry. We'll keep looking till we find them."

He sounded confident…but she saw his stricken gaze swerve to the living-room windows overlooking a thousand acres of pastures, hayfields and pine forest and knew exactly what he was thinking.

It wouldn't take long for two little girls to become disoriented in the snow. To fall. To find comfort in that soft, fluffy blanket of white…

She spun around and came face to face with Betty. "I can't find the twins. Please—help me search the house."

The two of them methodically searched every hiding place, then Abby grabbed her coat and boots. "Turn on all of the lights so they can see the house if they're outside. You stay here in case they come back, and I'm going out to help Jess."

Abby raced out to the horse barn where she found Jess ransacking the tack room and laundry, checking every nook and cranny.

"I'll check the hay stall. They have a fort in there." She ran to the hay stall and pulled open the sliding door. "Girls? Are you in here? Bella! Sophie!"

Nothing stirred.

She reached between the bales that had been stacked wider apart to create a little fort, then pulled some of them away for a better look. She pivoted back toward the aisle, defeated. "I thought for sure they would be in there."

Jess went on to the other barn and the machine shed, while Abby checked every stall. Every storage closet.

It was fully dark outside now. Her heart hammering in her chest, Abby started toward the indoor arena. Surely they wouldn't have dared to go into that cavernous, dark place, when they were too short to reach the light switches. Would they?

She heard a door creak open behind her and

the puppy came down the aisle, all tail wags and kisses as he bounced against her. Then Betty appeared, bundled up in a heavy coat with her cane in her hand. "I thought the pup might help if the girls are hiding."

Abby said a silent prayer as she opened the arena door and switched on the banks of overhead lights. It was cold out here as the thermostat was always turned off overnight. Even with the lights, the corners were dark and foreboding.

Poofy raced past her, running in ever-widening circles in the arena. Then he stopped. Cocked his head. And flew over the stack of hay where the kittens usually hid. He scrambled up the bales and poked his head into a space, wagging his tail.

Whispering yet another prayer, Abby hoped he'd found the girls and not a pile of sleepy kittens. "Bella! Sophie! Come out here, right now. Everyone is worried about you."

The puppy pawed at the hay and whined, and eventually the girls appeared, their hats askew and their faces streaked with tears. "We don't wanna go away," Sophie cried. "Don't make us."

Abby grabbed her cell phone from her jacket pocket and sent Jess a text, then rushed over and enveloped them in an embrace. "Dear Lord, thank You so much," she whispered as she led them back to the warmth of the horse barn.

She knelt in front of them and brushed off the

hay clinging to their jackets, then pulled them into another embrace when they started to sob. But what could she promise them, when no one here knew what the future would hold? "Sweeties, your Uncle Jess and Grandma Betty will always love you. You know that, don't you?"

Betty came up beside them and Abby looked up at her. "I don't know what this was all about, but it's going to be the happiest Christmas ever now that we've found them."

"I think I know," Betty said with a heavy sigh. "And I'm afraid this was all my fault."

Back at the house, Betty started a kettle of hot water for cocoa while Abby gave the girls a warm bath and put on their pajamas. When they came back, Betty settled them at the table where she had cookies and cocoa set out.

Jess still looked shaken. He lingered at the table for just a few minutes, then paced the kitchen before going back to his office.

Abby started to go after him, but Betty shook her head. She waited until the girls were done and wandered into the living room to play a game.

"I think he just needs a little time alone." Betty looked over her shoulder, then lowered her voice. "This whole situation was my fault. I was upset this afternoon, so I went to talk to Jess about Lindsey and that awful time she left the girls alone for so long." She glanced over her shoulder again. "I think the girls overheard me and it brought back their bad memories. I used to think they wanted nothing more than to go back home. But now I think they want to stay right here. They're still terrified of Lindsey's boyfriend, and of being abandoned...and who knows what else."

"Jess sure took this hard. Not that I blame him. I was terrified, too."

"He's a good man, Abby. And such a good dad to those girls."

Abby closed her eyes, recalling Betty's revelation about how Jess's father had cruelly, relentlessly blamed Jess and his brothers for the death of their sister. Yet Jess had somehow overcome those old childhood wounds and fear of responsibility and had taken in two vulnerable little girls in need. And Betty was right. He'd become a loving substitute dad.

She'd seen evidence of it every single day, but their disappearance tonight must have been a harsh reminder of the sister he'd lost and the deep sense of guilt he must've shouldered ever since.

"Doesn't he understand that his sister's death wasn't his fault?"

"I'm sure that on an intellectual level he does." Betty gave Abby a sad smile. "His mother tried to get through to all three boys when they were young. I tried, too. But the trauma was just too devastating to those sweet, caring little boys, and I think it changed them all forever. Some wounds are just too deep to heal."

Chapter Twenty-Four

Darkness had already fallen and a glittering sweep of stars filled the sky when Betty, Abby and Jess slipped into their usual pew for the Christmas Eve service. A few minutes later, Darla and Don slid in on Betty's other side.

Countless candles flickered across the front of the church, on the deep sills of the stained-glass windows and on the six-foot-high brass candlesticks at the ends of each pew.

When the organist began playing "O Little Town of Bethlehem" Jess closed his eyes and let the peace and beauty of this night wash over him. He was thankful from the depths of his heart that his family was here, safe and sound.

Last night at this time, he'd been terrified, jagged images of Heather's accident colliding with his fears that the twins might be freezing to death somewhere. That he'd failed them, too. Instead of reaching for faith, he'd succumbed to panic as the minutes ticked by.

But then, from somewhere in the depths of his memories, he'd remembered the verse his mother had quoted to him so many times. *In everything by prayer and supplication with thanksgiving let your requests be made known unto God. And the peace of God, which passeth all understanding, shall keep your hearts and minds through Christ Jesus.*

His mom had never lost her faith, even after Heather's death. But he had. Lost and angry and hurting, he'd turned away from it even though he'd gone through the motions of a churchgoer all these years.

But while searching desperately for the girls last night, he'd prayed hard for their safety, and the sense of calm and reassurance that had washed over him had given him hope when he'd only feared the worst.

After they'd been found safe and sound, he had sent up a heartfelt prayer of gratitude…grateful beyond measure that they'd been found.

Now, sitting next to Abby in the candlelit church, he felt the warmth of her arm next to his, and knew there was something else he needed to pray about before it was too late. Before Abby was gone.

Maybe he'd been too weak to face the horror

of what he'd done, but Dad never admitted his responsibility for Heather's death. He'd cruelly heaped that guilt onto his young sons and he'd gone to his grave without admitting the truth.

If Jess could finally forgive him, could he finally be free of the past? Finally feel whole and worthy?

Abby pressed closer to him and looked up at him with such warmth and understanding in her eyes that he wondered if she could read his mind. That warmth seemed to radiate from her hand to his, and straight to his heart.

Please, Lord, help me let go of the anger and hurt and guilt that I've held on to for so long. Help me to forgive Dad, just as You have forgiven your believers…and please help me take the right path with Abby and the twins…

"Look," Abby whispered, giving his hand a squeeze and then releasing it. "The children are coming in."

Maura walked down the aisle with her little flock of twenty following along behind her. They all wore loose, flowing children's choir tunics with a red bow. The littlest ones were scanning the pews for their parents and waving proudly as they marched to the front of the church.

Betty nudged his other side. "Isn't that just the sweetest thing? Here come Bella and Sophie!"

Betty waved to catch their attention and they both beamed proudly as they passed.

The older children took turns reciting their memorized verses from the Christmas story, interspersed with songs sung by the younger ones, with Maura kneeling in front of them to coach them along.

And then Sophie and Bella stepped ahead of the group, holding hands.

Abby sat forward. "Oh, my word," she whispered. "Look."

He leaned forward, too, and slipped his hand into hers again as the twins began to sing "Away in a Manger" in their high, clear voices. With their pale blond hair and the white tunics, they looked like little angels.

By the time they finished, his eyes were burning and his heart felt too full for his chest, and it was all he could do to just stay in his pew and not rush up to envelop them in an embrace.

Family. He'd once feared the thought of such responsibility. He'd decided it was better to be alone. But if the twins had come to him to teach him a lesson about love and caring and facing that risk, they'd done it ten times over.

Maybe it was time to finally do what he should have done years ago, even if he failed.

Back at home, Betty, Darla and Abby headed straight for the kitchen. The standing rib roast had gone into the oven on Low before church, and the side dishes had been prepared ahead of time.

Betty shooed the twins away from the oven door, then popped a nine-by-twelve-inch pan of scalloped potatoes in next to the roast. "Doesn't that smell good?"

Sophie and Bella nodded vigorously and edged toward the three-tier coconut cake on the counter. "That looks like a snowflake cake," Bella said. "Can we have some?"

Abby smiled. "Of course, but that's for dessert. We'll eat in an hour, then open our presents. Afterward, we can have dessert. Does that work for you?"

Bella's face fell.

"In the meantime, I know it's early. But if you want to get out of those dresses, there just might be some brand new Christmas pajamas on your beds."

Darla's face lit up. "I saw just the thing online—matching pajamas for an entire family. Can you imagine Don and Jess in Santa pajamas?"

Jess strolled into the kitchen. "Actually, no. Now Don, on the other hand…"

Abby laughed at the thought. Her dad might have softened up a lot since meeting Darla, but she couldn't imagine him ever giving in on that score. "Good luck with that, Darla."

From across the kitchen Jess's gaze locked on

hers. A little shiver of awareness slid through her, despite all of her resolutions. All of her plans. The plane reservations she'd made so she could start her new life—even if it meant facing a wrenching sense of loss at leaving this family behind.

He tipped his head toward the living room. "Can I talk to you for a minute? It won't take long."

Mystified, she set aside the pot holder in her hand and followed him to his office, where he closed the door and then turned to face her.

"Are you giving me the boot? On Christmas Eve?"

"Not quite." He pulled her into an embrace and tucked her head beneath his chin. So close that she could feel the beat of his heart.

"I probably shouldn't say this," he began. "But—"

Abby felt a flicker of hope come to life in her heart.

"Twelve years ago I failed to tell you something, and I'm not making that mistake again. I just want you to know the truth."

She held her breath.

"I loved you all those years ago, and I was too blind to admit it. I don't think I ever stopped." He pulled her closer again. "But I will not hold you back. You don't belong in the middle of nowhere on some ranch. You've got an amazing life ahead of you. A doctorate. A life of important research. You need to follow your dreams. Make us all proud of what you become."

She melted against him. "But that's just the thing. I can't."

"Of course you can."

"No. If I leave here, I'll be leaving everyone I love. You, the girls, my dad and everyone else."

"But you got that acceptance letter. How can you walk away from that?"

"Actually, I—"

"Jess! Abby!" Betty's voice came from far away. "We're ready to eat. I need Jess to carve the roast."

"Guess we'd better go," Abby said with a little laugh. "You've got one impatient grandma with very bad timing."

He followed her to the kitchen, but caught her hand as she passed under the arched doorway and glanced upwards. "Not so fast."

She followed his gaze. Drew in a sharp breath, well aware that everyone seemed to be watching.

Mistletoe.

Jess smiled down at her, then swept her into a kiss that sent sparks rocketing to her toes and made her heart feel ready to burst.

When he finally released her, she blinked as the family around them cheered and Betty shot her a knowing look. "About time," she said, her eyes twinkling.

Bella and Sophie looked at each other in shock, then at Jess and Abby, their eyes filled with wonder.

"Santa did it," Sophie whispered. "He really did!"

"Or it was all of my prayers," Betty said with a smile. "But however this happened, these two finally got it right."

Abby rested her head against Jess's shoulder as they sat together looking at the Christmas-tree lights. Everyone else had gone to bed by midnight, and now they were alone at last.

"I'll never forget this Christmas Eve," she said softly, turning her head to look at him. "It was so exciting to see the girls opening their presents—I thought they'd never go to sleep tonight. And I'm so glad you all welcomed Dad and Darla. It made my day complete."

"They're like family now." He smiled down at her. "I hope they'll always be able to join us here."

She felt his phone vibrating in his front pocket. He lifted it out to look at the screen and froze at the number displayed, then pressed the speaker button.

"Jess? This is Lindsey. Uh…my stepmom is

visiting me 'cause it's Christmas, and we need to ask you something."

Abby could feel his heart hammering against his ribs and sensed the wave of sorrow coursing through him at the sound of that voice.

"If you wanted to speak to the girls, they went to bed quite a while ago. I'm sorry."

"That's okay." Lindsey's voice reflected no regret. "I know I said I would come get them…but I couldn't."

She sounded disjointed, somehow. Her flat affect set off warning bells in Abby's head.

Lindsey's stepmother took over the phone. "Hello, Jess? This is Tara. I know you've had to take care of the girls way too long. I'm sorry about that."

Jess sat forward with a jerk. "No. No, it's fine."

"I travel a great deal for my career. I couldn't have taken them. Especially not at my age."

Like Lindsey, Tara had never once called to check on the twins since they'd come to Montana, and the brittle edge to her voice suggested that she would never have been eager to take in her step-grandchildren in any case.

"They're doing well here," Jess said. "We're very, very glad to have them."

"Good." Tara cleared her throat. "Because apparently Lindsey has spent the past year in and out of rehab. She and I were never very close, and of course with privacy laws no one could contact me until she finally allowed it in early November."

"Well, that explains a lot," Abby whispered to Jess.

His mouth flattened to a grim line. "How is she doing?"

"I tried bringing her home with me to San Diego, but that didn't last long. Now she's in a new facility near my house. It's very well-known, and I've… I've been trying to be more involved in her life. She has no contact with her dad, and I haven't been a very good stepmom all these years."

Abby felt her insides start to twist into a knot. If this call was about sending the girls back to a mother struggling with addiction—surely not—Jess needed to find a way to keep them safe right here in Montana. Abby slid her hand into his and squeezed.

"There's no way she can raise those girls," Tara continued. "She's still so young and way too fragile, and I think this is going to be a long road. Eventually, she wants to try college. But she says she'd be completely overwhelmed if she had to take the twins back."

Jess's eyes locked on Abby's and she bit her lower lip, her sympathy for the troubled girl mingling with a sudden flare of hope.

"She's sure?" he said slowly. "Absolutely sure?"

"Her counselor and a social worker have spent a

lot of time talking with us. We all agree that dragging out this situation isn't fair to young children who should have a stable and permanent home." Tara hesitated. "I hate to ask, since you've already had the twins for so long. But the social worker says you should be our first choice for adoption. Lindsey says she would like that, if you're willing."

Abby felt like jumping with joy. Instead, she threaded her arm through Jess's elbow and squeezed tight. He looked at her, his eyebrows raised, and she nodded emphatically.

"Yes. Absolutely."

Tara breathed a sigh of relief into the phone. "Thank you, Jess. I do think it's best if they're adopted by family. You'll be hearing from the social worker."

Long after the phone call ended, Abby gripped Jess's hand, still too relieved and excited to speak.

"What a Christmas," Jess said in wonder. He turned to her and cradled her face in his hands. "I got everything I could ever hope for. And far, far more. At least, I hope so."

Her heart stumbled, and the world around them seemed to still, coalescing into one breathless, expectant moment.

Their eyes met, locked, and then his mouth kicked up into the half smile she loved so much. "I know you have big plans for your life. I won't interfere with that. But we nearly made the right decision years ago, and then we got it all wrong," he said softly. "This time, I want to get this right."

She couldn't speak. She could barely breathe.

"I'll wait forever if there's a chance that you'll say *yes* to me someday. I don't know how it can ever work, or when, but…"

"But it can. And my answer is *yes*. A thousand times, *yes*." She pulled him into a long, sweet kiss. "I stayed up late last night looking at other options. I didn't even know such a thing existed, but one of the most prestigious universities in my field offers an online PhD program—one that only requires a number of weeklong, on-campus seminars during the year. It would work, Jess. I know it would."

There were no words that could convey what she felt about him, the girls, or the future they could share. He was everything she'd ever hoped for. Everything she'd thought she would never find.

And when he kissed her, she kissed him right back with all of the love in her heart.

Epilogue

Christmas morning dawned with an intensely blue sky and brilliant sunshine that turned the ranch into a sparkling wonderland of glittering snow and diamond-like icicles hanging from the eaves and every tree branch.

Last year, Christmas had been quiet, with just Jess and Betty sharing gifts and having Christmas dinner together.

This year was so much more—the house filled with so much laughter and joy that Jess felt as if his heart could burst. He'd finished his morning chores early, and after the Christmas Day church service, everyone returned to the ranch, where Betty, Darla and Abby all pitched in to prepare dinner while Jess and Don played board games with the girls on the floor in front of the crackling fire in the fireplace.

The puppy, with a big red bow around his neck, romped across the board scattering the pieces, and so they started once again, but this time on the coffee table. With soft instrumental Christmas music playing and the towering Christmas tree sparkling with its thousand little lights, Jess sat back and just drew it all in. Was it even possible to feel this much love?

How things had changed…with the arrival of the twins, with Don and Darla now a part of the family. And Abby.

Especially Abby.

"Play, Uncle Jess," Bella chirped. "It's your turn."

He eyed the board, deciding on a play that wouldn't jeopardize either of the girl's tokens, then made his move.

Poofy raced up to the coffee table, jumped on top and skidded across the playing board, landing in Jess's lap, his wagging tail a blur of motion. "You rascal," Jess said sternly, trying not to laugh as he hugged the pup and set him down again.

"He wants to play, too." Sophie giggled. "But he's a wigglepuss."

"That he is," Don said with a grin. "Which means he's perfect for two little girls."

Abby, Betty and Darla joined them in the living room, each wearing a bright red apron with twinkling Christmas trees over their church clothes.

"Dinner is ready," Abby announced, as she untied her apron. "But first I'd like to take pictures of everyone in front of the fireplace. This is a very, very special day."

She lifted an eyebrow and looked at Jess, and he nodded.

"I need to ask the girls a question," he said. "But first I have one more present for Abby. If she'll back up just a couple feet."

He waited until she stood beneath the archway leading into the kitchen, grinned and pointed up at the mistletoe. "I want to see if that will work a second time. What do you think, Bella and Sophie—will it?"

They giggled and clapped their hands. "Try, Uncle Jess!" they shouted in unison.

He went to stand in front of her and withdrew a small white box from his pocket. He opened it in front of her, revealing a three-quarter-carat solitaire glittering on a slender gold band.

Abby gasped. "It's…it's beautiful!"

"It was my mother's engagement ring," he said quietly. "My dad always said that his oldest son should use it."

She gingerly lifted the ring from the velvet lining. With a bit of pressure, it slid onto her finger. "Oh, Jess," she breathed. "I never expected this today. Or ever."

"I just wish I could have given it to you twelve years ago." He cleared his throat. "You can have it resized and reset in another style, if you want."

She shook her head and looked up at him with shining eyes. "I wouldn't change a thing."

Amid clapping and shouts of congratulations,

he pulled her into a long, sweet kiss, then glanced over at the twins. "How about that—the mistletoe still works!"

Laughing, the girls ran to him and hugged them both, their eyes shining.

He exchanged glances with Abby, knelt down and pulled the girls into his arms, and chose his words carefully. "You've been with us at the ranch for a long time, and we all love you very, very much. Well, we got a call last night, and now I need to ask you something."

Sophie's eyes filled with fear and sudden tears, and he wondered just how much she remembered of her life before coming to Montana. "We hafta leave? I don't *want* to," she whispered.

"You're sending us away?" Bella's lower lip trembled. "What about Poofy and Lollipops and Gramma? And you, Uncle Jess? And Abby?"

"What would you think about staying here forever and ever?"

Sophie launched into his embrace and wrapped her arms tightly around his neck, sobbing.

Bella hung back, her eyes wide. "Did our momma die?"

"No, sweetheart. But she brought you here because she knew she couldn't take care of you, and she wants you to have a forever home here, where you can have ponies and puppies and even more people to love you."

"W-will we ever see her again?"

"She will always be welcome here. Always. Maybe next summer she'll come for a visit, and next Christmas, too."

Bella nodded, a smile lighting up her face, and she threw her arms around him. When he rose, Betty kissed him, too, with tears streaming down her face.

And then Abby stepped into his arms once again for another sweet kiss.

"A Christmas to remember," she whispered as they walked to the dining room for dinner. "And the start of many, many more."

* * * * *

If you loved this story, be sure to check out the miniseries Aspen Creek Crossroads

Winter Reunion
Second Chance Dad
The Single Dad's Redemption
An Aspen Creek Christmas
Falling For The Rancher

*from bestselling author Roxanne Rustand
Available now from Love Inspired!*

*Find more great reads at
www.LoveInspired.com*

Dear Reader,

Thank you so much for joining me as I begin my *Rocky Mountain Ranch* series for Love Inspired. I hope you enjoyed *Montana Mistletoe*.

For those of you who followed my previous *Aspen Creek Crossroads* series, thank you! If you read the final book, *Falling for the Rancher*, you may have noticed the mention of that hero in this book. It was such fun adding just a bit of a connection while beginning a new, unrelated series!

My husband and I live on an acreage with horses, some rescued cats and two big rescue dogs who consider themselves lap puppies. I love writing stories set in small towns and ranch country, and also love writing about the complexities and connections of multi-generational families…and how my characters must overcome conflicts, old wounds and challenges to reach a place where they can finally enjoy an abundant, faith-filled life.

I love to hear from readers, and promise to answer.

Snail mail: Roxanne Rustand, Box 2550, Cedar Rapids, Iowa 52406

Email: via www.roxannerustand.com.

Facebook: www.facebook.com/roxanne.rustand.

Wishing you every blessing now and in the coming year,

Roxanne

Get 4 FREE REWARDS!

We'll send you 2 FREE Books plus 2 FREE Mystery Gifts.

Love Inspired® Suspense books feature Christian characters facing challenges to their faith... and lives.

FREE
Value Over
$20

YES! Please send me 2 FREE Love Inspired® Suspense novels and my 2 FREE mystery gifts (gifts are worth about $10 retail). After receiving them, if I don't wish to receive any more books, I can return the shipping statement marked "cancel." If I don't cancel, I will receive 4 brand-new novels every month and be billed just $5.24 each for the regular-print edition or $5.74 each for the larger-print edition in the U.S., or $5.74 each for the regular-print edition or $6.24 each for the larger-print edition in Canada. That's a savings of at least 13% off the cover price. It's quite a bargain! Shipping and handling is just 50¢ per book in the U.S. and 75¢ per book in Canada*. I understand that accepting the 2 free books and gifts places me under no obligation to buy anything. I can always return a shipment and cancel at any time. The free books and gifts are mine to keep no matter what I decide.

Choose one: ☐ **Love Inspired® Suspense**
Regular-Print
(153/353 IDN GMY5)

☐ **Love Inspired® Suspense**
Larger-Print
(107/307 IDN GMY5)

Name (please print)

Address   Apt. #

City   State/Province   Zip/Postal Code

Mail to the **Reader Service:**
IN U.S.A.: P.O. Box 1341, Buffalo, NY 14240-8531
IN CANADA: P.O. Box 603, Fort Erie, Ontario L2A 5X3

Want to try two free books from another series? Call 1-800-873-8635 or visit www.ReaderService.com.

*Terms and prices subject to change without notice. Prices do not include applicable taxes. Sales tax applicable in N.Y. Canadian residents will be charged applicable taxes. Offer not valid in Quebec. This offer is limited to one order per household. Books received may not be as shown. Not valid for current subscribers to Love Inspired Suspense books. All orders subject to approval. Credit or debit balances in a customer's account(s) may be offset by any other outstanding balance owed by or to the customer. Please allow 4 to 6 weeks for delivery. Offer available while quantities last.

Your Privacy—The Reader Service is committed to protecting your privacy. Our Privacy Policy is available online at www.ReaderService.com or upon request from the Reader Service. We make a portion of our mailing list available to reputable third parties that offer products we believe may interest you. If you prefer that we not exchange your name with third parties, or if you wish to clarify or modify your communication preferences, please visit us at www.ReaderService.com/consumerschoice or write to us at Reader Service Preference Service, P.O. Box 9062, Buffalo, NY 14240-9062. Include your complete name and address.

LIS18

Get 4 FREE REWARDS!

We'll send you 2 FREE Books <u>plus</u> 2 FREE Mystery Gifts.

Bad Boy Rancher
Karen Rock

Love Songs and Lullabies
Amy Vastine

Harlequin® Heartwarming™ Larger-Print books feature traditional values of home, family, community and most of all—love.

FREE Value Over **$20**

YES! Please send me 2 FREE Harlequin® Heartwarming™ Larger-Print novels and my 2 FREE mystery gifts (gifts worth about $10 retail). After receiving them, if I don't wish to receive any more books, I can return the shipping statement marked "cancel." If I don't cancel, I will receive 4 brand-new larger-print novels every month and be billed just $5.49 per book in the U.S. or $6.24 per book in Canada. That's a savings of at least 19% off the cover price. It's quite a bargain! Shipping and handling is just 50¢ per book in the U.S. and 75¢ per book in Canada*. I understand that accepting the 2 free books and gifts places me under no obligation to buy anything. I can always return a shipment and cancel at any time. The free books and gifts are mine to keep no matter what I decide.

161/361 IDN GMY3

Name (please print)

Address   Apt. #

City   State/Province   Zip/Postal Code

Mail to the **Reader Service:**
IN U.S.A.: P.O. Box 1341, Buffalo, NY 14240-8531
IN CANADA: P.O. Box 603, Fort Erie, Ontario L2A 5X3

Want to try two free books from another series! Call 1-800-873-8635 or visit www.ReaderService.com.

*Terms and prices subject to change without notice. Prices do not include applicable taxes. Sales tax applicable in N.Y. Canadian residents will be charged applicable taxes. Offer not valid in Quebec. This offer is limited to one order per household. Books received may not be as shown. Not valid for current subscribers to Harlequin Heartwarming Larger-Print books. All orders subject to approval. Credit or debit balances in a customer's account(s) may be offset by any other outstanding balance owed by or to the customer. Please allow 4 to 6 weeks for delivery. Offer available while quantities last.

Your Privacy—The Reader Service is committed to protecting your privacy. Our Privacy Policy is available online at www.ReaderService.com or upon request from the Reader Service. We make a portion of our mailing list available to reputable third parties that offer products we believe may interest you. If you prefer that we not exchange your name with third parties, or if you wish to clarify or modify your communication preferences, please visit us at www.ReaderService.com/consumerschoice or write to us at Reader Service Preference Service, P.O. Box 9062, Buffalo, NY 14240-9062. Include your complete name and address.

HW18

READERSERVICE.COM

Manage your account online!
- Review your order history
- Manage your payments
- Update your address

> ### We've designed the
> ### Reader Service website
> ### just for you.

Enjoy all the features!
- Discover new series available to you, and read excerpts from any series.
- Respond to mailings and special monthly offers.
- Browse the Bonus Bucks catalog and online-only exculsives.
- Share your feedback.

Visit us at:
ReaderService.com

RS16R